The OCD Games

A Christmas Novella

Kayla Krantz

This is a work of fiction. All of the characters and events portrayed in this novel are either products of the author's imagination or are used fictitiously.

The OCD Games

Cover by BetiBup33
https://thebookcoverdesigner.com/?s=BetiBup33

Edited by Raven Heidrich

ISBN: **978-1-950530-29-8**
First Edition March 2022
Library of Congress Control Number: 2018910858

https://authorkaylakrantz.com/

1.

I STARE AT the door set into the gothic archway of the church a moment before my hand wraps around the simple brass doorknob. There's a conflict between the doorway and the knob—simple versus complex, like me in a way. At eye level, sits a wreath, full and fresh—not one of the fake ones bought at a craft store, reeking of scented pinecones, but real and alive. It hangs here, a bit of festivity to spruce up the boring door and the even more boring reason I'm here.

Okay, support group isn't *always* boring. Sometimes, I can relate to the others, and when I've had a rough week, it's almost cleansing, like I'm actually going to a sermon here rather than into the basement. Lately though, the process has felt a bit repetitive, something I *have* to go to rather than something I want to. More often than not, I sit in the chair, drowning out all the things happening around me with thoughts of where else I could be and what else I could be doing.

I push the thoughts away and make my way inside. As usual, there are five chairs in the circle—four for the people like me and one for the support leader, Destiny, who I suppose is also like me. She's a woman of about thirty-five with a compulsive need to do things in a certain order. According to her, she's had the same routine every day for the last decade and hasn't detoured once. I try to imagine how that could be possible but find that any extended time put into thoughts of her life makes me sad.

Even though we're *both* affected with OCD, I feel bad for her. I can't imagine living the same day over and over again. Doesn't it ever get dull? I don't know why I'm so judgmental. I'm not one to talk. I sit in the plastic chair by the window like I always do, chewing my nails down to the quick. OCD and anxiety is a cruel mixture sometimes, but this seat helps. It's the only one that offers a good look outside, at the fresh snow that's just beginning to fall. Outside, I can *feel* the Christmas spirit, but in here…?

I only feel depression, my reasons for being here once a week. There is no cheering up the feeling of this basement no matter how many Christmas decorations Destiny uses. The other three chairs fill in as my brother and sisters in compulsion—Brayden, Serena, and Alice—file into their respective seats. I nod and smile at each of them, but my mind is divided with thoughts as Destiny begins the meeting. All I can think about is how I usually go to work directly after support group but today, that's not an option.

Today presents something that people like me are completely uncomfortable with—change. I try to ignore the uncomfortable wiggle in my stomach that that thought alone creates and glance at Destiny. I see her lips moving but hear none of the words coming out. It's like everything is under water as I run through my thoughts. What in the world would *Destiny* do if she were in my shoes? How would she go on if someone told her she could no longer lead these support meetings?

"Erica!" her voice pops my bubble and pulls me back to attention.

My eyes widen as I focus on her. I don't even have it in me to *pretend* that I've been listening.

"How are you doing this week?" she asks.

I sigh. This week has been heated, dreadful, and the free time has given me too big of an opportunity to fall back into my habits; the bad ones that this group is intended to stop. Even though this is the place to admit all that, I don't want to. I've always considered myself the strongest of all of us. I guess we always see ourselves as the hero of our own stories, but being honest leaves me feeling less than everyone else…even though I know I shouldn't.

"Good," I lie and run my fingers together three times.

Destiny watches the tiny movement, and as soon as I see her eyes on my hands, I tuck them together, which earns a frown from her. "Erica? This is a *safe* place. You don't have to feel ashamed."

Now I feel worse than I had a moment ago. I've been with this group for a little less than a year now, so her words are not news to me. I pretend to smile at the comment anyway, like no one has ever offered such wisdom. The smile doesn't last. "I-it's been a rough week," I admit, dropping my chin. "I lost my job because well…"

Serena, seated in the chair next to me, reaches out to place her hand on my knee. The touch is encouraging, and I appreciate the effort, but I wonder how long I have to wait before it's considered acceptable to move her hand away.

"I…take too long in my morning routine, and I was almost always late to work," I admit. "I tried getting up early on multiple occasions, but it seemed like that just made it worse."

Serena's lips pull downward at my words, and her tiny fingers grip tighter. I wince and take the opportunity to pull her hand off. She gives me an apologetic look, and I wonder if she realizes how strong she really is.

"I'm sorry, but why wouldn't they just accommodate your schedule?" she asks.

I shrug, eyes dragging from her to the floor. I have a safe box in the back of my mind where I try to hold onto questions like that, questions that could stress me out or cause me pain from a situation long past. Hers is one I had kept under lock and key. Now it's free and not just for me to ponder, but for an entire room of people.

"Have they no compassion? It's almost Christmas!" Alice chimes in her disgust of the normal world outside this room. Beside her, Brayden nods along.

My eyes stay fixated on the same floorboard as I listen to them all voice their opinion. Wanting the subject to change, I add, "I've been working on my yoga and drawing to help me clear my mind."

Destiny bobs her head and writes something on the pad of paper on her lap. "Good, that's good. Anything in particular?"

I shake my head. "They're all uh…abstract, I guess," I murmur, thinking of the charcoal shadow drawing I had done in my last class.

They give me a round of applause, but I wonder if I really deserve it. Then Destiny's attention turns away. "Brayden, you're awfully quiet today. How has your week been?"

I'm glad to feel the spotlight fall off of me. I smile at Brayden encouragingly even though I don't hear a word he says as I go back to tuning the world out. I handle everyone in the same manner, and I'm nothing but grateful when support group is over this time. I pick up my bag and try to beat everyone to the door like I do every week. Serena, filled with bouncing curiosity—the same kind you see in five-year-olds—stops me at the door.

"Hey, I'm really sorry to hear about your job," she says, hand on my shoulder. *Why does she keep touching me?*

I shrug it off because I don't know what else to do. "It's okay. It's not like I planned to work there forever, anyway." I don't wait for Serena's reply before I walk ahead, going through the door and out into the cold December day.

My words to her are the truth. I hated the job. It was one routine that I am *not* sad to see go. Yet, I'm sad just the same.

2.

*M*Y FOOTSTEPS ECHO *strangely as I walk down the hall. Each thud seems to bounce up off the floor and around the walls, filling my ears before fading and returning with the next step I take. There's a chill running down the length of my spine that warns me of impending danger, but I don't understand it at all. I'm at work, a place I've been a thousand times before, yet something's different. I can feel it in the air.*

I walk on, attempting to shrug off the sensation, but it nags harder when my boss' voice catches me as soon as I pass by the entrance to her office. "Erica, can I speak to you for a moment, please?"

I peer inside. Her face is anything but welcoming, and instead of sitting in the chair in front of her desk, I wish I would've pretended that I hadn't heard her. That I had just kept walking down the hall.

"You're fired," she says, no greeting or prologue to start it off.

I gasp and sit up so fast that I nearly bash my forehead into the lamp hanging above my bed. It used to hang higher, but the water damage in my ceiling has caused it to lower by an inch or two—just enough to be in my way. I swat at it bitterly, vowing to move it with the knowledge that it'll most likely never happen. Above my bed also happens to be the center of the room. Since the lamp is the only thing on my ceiling, it *has* to maintain its position in the exact middle…even if the ceiling gives out. That is, unless I decide to get three identical lamps and hang one in each corner, but who has the time?

Not to mention the money.

With a sigh, I swipe my fox-colored hair out of my eyes and make my way to the bathroom. My freckled cheeks are flushed from the nightmares of my recent life event, and I allow myself just a moment to laugh at my reflection in the bathroom mirror before I go to work, cleaning myself up. Cold water directly from the faucet feels like Heaven on my skin. Once I'm in order, I put my makeup on, starting with my eyes, despite the constant criticism that my best friend, Kara, gives me for my lack of makeup skills.

She's not here now, I think with another laugh as I put my face together in my special backwards way.

With that done, I turn on the faucet to rinse off the mascara smeared on my thumb. After drying my hands, I turn back to the sink to wash them two more times. My morning routine takes a good amount of time to get through, and sometimes, I hate myself for being this way, barely having the energy to continue it, but also knowing that things can't go any other way. I can't imagine how much I could get done in a day without my rituals, how many hours would be freed if I was just *normal.*

Maybe I could learn a new language…or keep a *job.*

Most days though, I'm no-fear-cavalier. I take it in stride, right down to Kara's never-ending jabs, just as Destiny tells me to do. Besides, today's not the day to get hung up on anything. Even though it's only been two days since support group, and the beginning of my search for a new job, I already have an interview. My ball of anxiety makes it hard to muster up the chipper attitude I could otherwise approach today with. It hadn't been tough to interest a potential employer so quickly—with my experience, I have quite a few options, but I chose something simple to make it easier, a cashier at a small convenience store.

After the most intricate of my routine is complete, I ruffle my ginger hair with my fingers, trying to add volume to it before I groan and leave the bathroom. I stand by the front door and turn the lights in the living room on and off exactly three times before leaving the house and locking the door. I try to drag myself off the porch to my car but only make it two steps before I'm back, checking the locks a second and third time. Finally satisfied, I make it to my car and sit in the driver's seat, taking a deep breath through my nose.

My routine shatters here—I'm entering new territory, a situation completely unfamiliar to me. I could throw up. I *feel* the bile in the back of my throat as I pull out of my driveaway, but I force it away. If I puke, I'll have to go home and brush my teeth three more times, and I can't afford the time if I plan to not be late.

My hands clench around the steering wheel, though I'm not conscious of them doing so. The whiteness of the skin over my knuckles shows just how tense I am, and I try to talk myself out of my anxiety, to convince myself that it's ridiculous to feel this way. Surely, normal people don't…it's just an entry level position that *anyone* can apply for, but I'm terrible at convincing myself.

Talking myself into getting out of the car once I arrive takes some work, and I trip over my feet only once on my way inside the store. *That* I actually consider to be a victory. It's small and gives me the motivation to find the manager, Greg, who greets me with a capricious smile on his face that reminds me of a shark.

He leads me through the store for a long period of time before bothering to ask, "You're Erica Mills, right?" as we head into a small office at the back of the store which fits him, his desk, a lamp, and a chair. He goes to close the door, but I hold a hand out, and he leaves it cracked. The feeling of claustrophobia sits in my stomach like acid.

I nod, trying to hide how sick this room makes me by tucking a strand of red hair behind my ear as I sit rigidly in the uncomfortable chair in front of his desk.

"Well, your resume is impressive. If hired, what do you believe you'd bring to the team?"

"Uh, well, I…" I frown and struggle for words, knowing how bad it looks to get hung up on the *first* question. Inside, I kick myself. *Why* didn't I prepare? For all my obsessive tendencies, I had not had the foresight to think about possible interview questions. *Idiot.* "Order," I spit out stupidly, staring at him as if it makes sense.

He waits, clearly waiting for a follow-up explanation that I don't have, and plasters another smile to his face but doesn't seem thrown off by my stupidity. "Okay, well, what are your strengths?"

"I'm neat and capable. I know what I want and how to get it," I say with confidence that seems misplaced with the impression I've already made with question number one. *Idiot,* I chant again, dragging out the word in my head.

"All right, Miss Mills. One last question for you—when can you start?"

My face must brighten at the question because the smile he gives is painfully wide. Or maybe he just always looks like that. Who knows?

"As soon as possible," I say, hoping to not come off as desperate.

"I will see you tomorrow morning then, Erica. Glad to have you on board," Greg says and reaches across the desk to shake my hand.

Maybe there's such a thing as Christmas miracles after all.

3.

CLUTCHING THE PAPERS that Greg had given me, I sit in my car, running through proper breathing exercises again. My heart begins to calm down, though every time I try to begin reading the papers, it starts up again. I skip over the job duties portion and skim down to the dress code. I toss the paper into the seat beside me and adjust my mirrors before pulling out of the parking lot.

I text Kara to see if she's at home, then I go by our favorite café and fight down my wave of anxiety again to go inside and order a frappe for Kara and a cappuccino for myself. For some reason, I watch the cashier with extended interest—that probably makes me look like a weirdo from his point of view—but I can't help it.

The thought that this will be me tomorrow is a strange one.

"Have a nice day, ma'am," he says, bright smile on his face as he hands me back my change.

I blink and return the pleasantry, breaking out of my strange trance long enough to realize I've been staring too long. I turn away quickly and head through the door, two steaming cups of coffee in my hands, and make my way to the car. When I climb back into the driver's seat, I check my phone and see that there's a reply from Kara.

Kara: At work, baby doll.

Usually, that would've bummed me out because I hate the mall with a passion that only introverts can understand, but it works today. I need to find something acceptable to wear anyway, and she's my go-to person for everything fashionable, whether it be clothing or makeup.

I pull into one of the parking spaces farthest from the door and gather the coffee before making my way across the parking lot. Unlike the tiny parking lot of the convenience store that I now work at, this one has been salted, so it's not slippery.

Thankfully. It would be just like me to slip and spill both cups of coffee on myself.

I make it inside without incident and look at the map overview to find my way to the clothing store where Kara works. As soon as I go inside, I see her bent over the counter, blonde hair draped over her shoulder and snapping loudly on a pink piece of bubble gum.

When she turns and sees me, her red lips turn up into a smile, and she stands to her feet, eyes on the coffee in my hands. "Well, how'd it go?" she asks, eagerly accepting my offering.

"Good, good," I say. "I got the job."

"As I knew you would," she replies and tips back her head to down a big gulp of her coffee.

I wonder how she does it without burning herself, but when I take a sip of my own, I realize it's cooled considerably from the journey. "But now I need your help," I admit and pass her the paper with my new dress code on it.

"Hmm?" Kara asks, setting down her cup to pick up the paper. She skims it, and her lips curve into a smile again as she thrusts it down. "I've got the *perfect* outfit in mind for you."

"Uh-oh," I say and hold my coffee up to my chin, though I don't take a sip this time.

"No, uh-oh," she says and pries it from my hand before grasping my wrist and leading me toward the dressing rooms. "Wait here."

I stare at her with pleading eyes. I hate dressing rooms. They're cramped and tiny, not to mention the fact that I don't know if there are cameras in here or not. Sure, they say not, but you never quite know. My heart pounds as I wait for her to return, looking for hidden cameras and wishing I still had my coffee to sip on if for nothing more than a distraction from myself. I eye the tiny bench and take off my jacket before sitting on it.

At last, there comes a knock on the door, and Kara peeks her head inside. "Ready?" she asks.

I shrug, and she tosses a bundle of clothes into my arms, slamming the door shut behind her before I can protest her selection.

"I want to see it!" she says from the other side.

I sigh and finally look at what she's given me—a collared, white, button-down blouse and a black pencil skirt. The sight causes me to frown—it's too much like what I would've worn at my last job.

"This isn't an office job, Kara," I protest.

"And?" she asks. "You look smokin' in pencil skirts, and if you double check your list, a white collar shirt *is* a requirement, so stop complainin', and follow my advice, girl."

I'm out of arguments, so I oblige. Setting the clothing down on my jacket, I glance up at the corners of the tiny room again for cameras and give up, quickly stripping down to my underwear. I pull the new clothes into place, the stiff fabric sitting uncomfortably against my skin with the thought that I don't know *how* many people have tried these clothes on before me. Again, I try not to think of that as I button the shirt and look at myself in the mirror.

The outfit *does* look good on me, but it's not my style. I feel exposed, bare, for the way it hugs my figure. If I have my choice, I always pick clothes that are at least a size or two bigger than I am. The only drawback of having Kara do my shopping for me is that that is no longer an option. I twist my fingers into my hair and toss it over my shoulder to observe the collar against my skin. Then, I take the outfit off and repeat the process two more times, checking to see if the shirt and skirt skim my curves the same way they had the first time.

"Well? I'm waiting!" Kara's keen voice sounds from the other side of the door.

I look at my reflection again and brace myself to show her. I already know from experience that if I don't go out there willingly, she'll come *in*. I open the door with a pop and Kara is right in my face, hands straightening out the lumps on my shoulders and pulling the blouse down to get rid of any potential creases. Then, she takes a step back and looks me up and down like an artist evaluating a newly finished piece. Frowning, she comes toward me again and plucks the clip out of my hair, letting all the golden-orange locks flow free in a messy cascade.

"With the right shoes, you'll be *perfect!*" she squeals and claps excitedly.

"Thanks," I murmur and take my clip from her fingers.

"Hang on," she says and dashes off, presumably to find the shoes, and I turn to my reflection, trying to tame my mane back into the hold it had previously been in.

By the time I've finished, she returns with a shoe box, and I'm almost afraid to look inside. "There better not be high heels in here," I tease, raising an eyebrow.

Kara rolls her eyes. "Nope. Trust me. I learned a lesson the last time. They're flats. They're fashionable and reasonable, here," she says and takes the top off the box to show me as if she knows I don't believe her.

The shoes inside are small and black. She's right about one thing, they actually *are* reasonable. Under her encouraging stare, I pluck them free from the crinkly paper and sit down on the floor to pull the shoes on the best way I can with the pencil skirt constricting my thigh movement. Kara, noticing my struggle, drops to her knees to help me. As soon as they're on, she looks me up and down again and wolf whistles.

"You're marvelous, darling! Simply gorgeous," she gushes, using a fake accent like a Hollywood agent.

I chuckle and try to peel off the shoes in a hurry. "Thanks."

"That's what friends are for," she says, voice back to normal. "Now, go get dressed, and I'll find you a couple more pieces. Meet me where we left our coffee when you're done."

Nodding, I head back into the dressing room, gratefully stripping off the new clothes and replacing them with my own. I bundle them into my arms and meet Kara at the counter, dropping them next to my long abandoned cup of coffee.

"How much is this going to be?" I ask, reaching for my wallet after she bags the clothes.

Kara raises an eyebrow. "Nothing."

I pause. "Huh?"

"It's my treat, girl. The least I can do to start you off on the right foot."

"You can't do that!" I protest, frowning. Using Kara's discount is one thing, but having her pay for my clothes is another. I've never been the type who's comfortable with letting someone pay for my things…especially when I know those things probably cost a pretty penny.

"Why not? How many times have you bought me things?" she asks, taking a purposeful sip of her coffee, staring at me over the rim the entire time.

I sigh in defeat. She won't let me win this argument. "Fine, fine," I say at last.

This time, she smiles wide enough to show every one of her pearl white teeth beneath her coral red lips.

4.

WHEN I GET home, I spend a good portion of my evening just rearranging my clothes. Some of them go into the trash as I work out a section in my closet for my new work outfits. There are four in total and I shake my head, feeling worse for Kara's kindness than I know I should.

I'll pay her back, I think in my head. Of course, this isn't the first time I've thought it, but actually seeing everything firsthand strengthens the urge.

After everything is settled, I go through my extensive process to get ready for bed and settle in underneath my low hanging lamp, trying to ignore the fact that tomorrow will once again bring me a myriad of change.

I wake up from a dreamless, finicky sleep, feeling almost as if I hadn't slept at all, and swipe the lamp away to sit up. Groaning at a pain in the base of my spine, I get up and go directly to the bathroom to splash water on my face—the start of my typical routine. The only exception today is putting on my new work uniform. I sift through the outfits that Kara picked, but eventually settle on the one that I had already tried on with that logic that of all of them, it's the one I'm the most familiar with. I smooth down the white collar of the pressed shirt, wishing I would've remembered to wash it, and smile at my reflection, trying— unsuccessfully—to make my anxiety go away. The reflection smiling back at me does little to help because I can *see* the unease in the girl's eyes.

I wonder if other people can see that glint too or if I can only because I already know its there.

This will be good. I won't get fired this time, I promise myself, thinking of Kara's words and hoping that I really do look *that* good. Just for good measure, I repeat my own thoughts two more times, and on the last run through, I add, *Support group is helping, I will be normal.*

I pull the flats on and off my feet absently, and when my nerves are settled, I snag my purse off the table beside the front door and rush outside. Running through the proper procedure of locks and checks, I move to my car and think through my mantras, trying to keep my dumb cavalier cheer. I don't know how long I can make it last because the closer I get to my new job, the stronger the wave of anxiety rises. As I pull into the parking lot, the smile falls off my face, and I have a moment where I see myself with far too much clarity. I start to hyperventilate but convince myself it's ridiculous. Do I really want to give the impression that I'm nothing but a bag of nerves?

No, I don't.

Stalling for time, I adjust all my mirrors and let out a breath of air. A glance at the time tells me how close I'm cutting it. Nerves semi-ready for the situation ahead of me, I climb out of the safety of my car and move to close the door when I realize my purse is still sitting in the passenger seat.

I bend over to grab it when I feel hands grasp my hips. I scream, heart thudding in my chest, before I try and stand up, hitting my head on the roof of my car and slipping on the ice in my new flats. Wincing, I lift my hand to the back of my head and maneuver out of the car to see who's behind me. Laughter erupts, and I frown, feeling the heat in my cheeks as I glare at Kara who is doubled over to exaggerate the moment. Her long blonde hair hangs around her angular face as she struggles to regain herself.

"You scare so easy, girl!" she says.

"God!" I gasp and hold a hand over my heart, thankful that today I skipped out on getting a cup of coffee like I used to do before my office job. "My nerves are already on edge—you could've given me a heart attack!" I accuse, slamming my car door for emphasis.

"Ah, you lived," she says, wiping the tears from under her eyes before waving a dismissive hand at me. She tucks her hands into the pockets of her jacket, which I notice is unzipped enough to show the pink shirt underneath. 'This shirt only looks good because I'm wearing it," it boasts. Even in the coldest of weather she wants everyone to see her fashion choices…even if it means having to suffer to do so.

I laugh—the shirt is so Kara.

Kara smiles back and looks down at it, picking at the fabric of her jacket with her long pink nails to show a bigger slice of the writing. "I know, right? Perfection."

"There's one word for it," I say as we begin to walk up to the doors of the building. "What are you doing here anyway?"

"Just wanted to see you off on your big day!"

By the gleam in her eyes, today seems more like her first day than mine. "This isn't school, and you aren't my mom."

"Hmm. I wouldn't be so sure about that. I *did* pick out your outfit, if I do recall," she says and holds a finger mischievously to her lips.

"Little girls dress dolls too," I point out, smiling back at her.

Kara smiles and playfully punches me in the shoulder. "Who needs a mom when you have an awesomely wonderful best friend?"

"Can't argue with that logic."

"I hoped you wouldn't!"

Caught up in the laughter of our conversation, I don't feel the anxiety entering the store that I know would've choked me without her. In the moment, I think about reaching out to give her a huge hug but decide against it. How awkward of a notion when we just agreed she *wasn't* my mom.

Thankfully, the store is a lot calmer than it had been when I came for my interview. The less people I deal with, the easier it will be to downplay my OCD should I happen to find a new quirk to add to my routine while we're here. Once we fall silent, the worst of myself begins to rise up again when I remember that I'm going to have to go through today by myself. Kara can't stay by my side all day—if she did, it certainly wouldn't look good on my part.

Kara notices my frown and raises a perfect eyebrow in question.

"My anxiety feels like it's through the roof," I admit with a sigh.

Kara gives me a lips-too-tight smile, the kind that shows me she's trying to sympathize with a problem she's never had. "Tell you what. If you make it through the day, which I have faith you will, we'll go to a concert or something to celebrate on your first day off."

I sigh and reach up to tousle my carefully fixed hair only lamenting on what I've just done after the fact. No time to fix it now. I've never been a fan of crowded events, but it's always good to have something to look forward to. It makes the tough times the slightest bit easier to dredge through. "Sounds like a plan," I say to Kara and successfully keep the majority of my emotions out of those four words.

"Okay. Now, get to work," she orders, false seriousness in her voice. She stops in her steps and watches me expectantly to continue onward. She waves slightly and blows me a kiss before skewing off in a different direction to scope out my new workplace.

She's more excited to be here than I am, it seems. That thought keeps the smile on my face as I seek out my new boss. When our eyes meet, the shark smile comes to his face, and he greets me with a handshake.

"So, how much have you shopped here in the past?" Greg asks me after we leave his office and a mountain of completed paperwork behind.

"Uh, honestly? Not very often," I reply, expecting him to be disappointed.

He's not. We pass by a tiny room with a rickety fan spinning above a table beside a refrigerator. "This is the break room," he says and turns his attention to the collection of tiny lockers outside of the room.

Two of them are closed with tiny combination locks holding them shut, and another one is closed without anything to keep it that way. Greg opens this one and pulls out a tiny nametag and apron. He smiles at them before handing them to me. "Here is the rest of your uniform," he says then taps his finger on the door of the tiny locker. "And this will be your space here to put your purse or other personal belongings."

He eyes the purse I've forgotten is clutched beneath my arm, and reluctantly, I hand it to him. He sets it inside and pulls an extra lock off the top of the lockers, so high up that I hadn't even known it was there.

"The combination is 7-4-18," he informs me. "Try it."

I oblige and spin the lock three times to get all the numbers. Then repeat the process again and again. I actually like the device. The fact that it operates only if it is spun three times correctly resonates with the compulsive part of my personality.

Now you've really lost your mind if you think inanimate objects are your friends, I think but don't show any kind of scathing on the outside as I finally latch the lock on the locker.

"Now, for a quick tour of the store," Greg says.

I don't argue, following a few steps behind him while trying to tie the apron in place. I don't want to ask Greg to do it for me because one, he most likely won't do it to my standards, and two, how awkward of a request that would be to my *boss* of all people. I get the knot secured before he notices my struggle. For being a stout man, he walks rather quickly and leads the way from the dairy section through the produce to the frozen food to the pet supplies and then to the tiny medicine section that's so pitiful I wouldn't call it a pharmacy department, but he does, so I stay quiet.

At last, we approach the front, and my spine straightens instantly, ready for a confrontation of some kind as my boss' gaze sweeps across the two registers and the cashiers on both of them. It's my first real look at my new coworkers, but suddenly, I feel too shy to look directly at either of them as if I'm afraid they'll bite me like a rabid dog if we accidentally make eye contact. My gaze shifts to the floor as my boss leads me to the closest register.

There's a blonde cashier at this one. Her hair is long and layered, and my first impression of her is that she'll have a less than stellar attitude about having a shadow. She surprises me with a warm smile, showing white teeth stained with a smudge of lipstick, and my uneasiness dissolves away. *She's just a human girl,* I tell myself. *Possibly an airhead, but a human one nonetheless.*

"Camilla, this is Erica," my boss introduces us. "She's going to shadow you today."

Camilla nods. "A new girl, how exciting!"

"I'll check in on you later, Erica," Greg promises. "I'll be in my office. Don't hesitate to find me if you have any questions or concerns."

"Thanks again," I say, forcing a tiny smile on my face and watch him walk away.

Then it's just me and Camilla, and I'm aware of how close together we are in the cramped little box provided by the register. I take a step backward, hoping I haven't already made her too uncomfortable, but Camilla is still smiling that wide lipstick-stained smile and claps her hands together like she's trying to get a toddler to be excited about eating his vegetables.

"This is awesome! I haven't had my own apprentice yet," she gushes, and that's all it takes to feel uneasy again.

Seems like a bit of an overreaction on her part, and all I can think of is high school. Of the cheerleaders who had a habit of dramatizing their every move. *She fits the type,* I smile at that but feel uncertain of how to respond. Camilla has only given me an impression of kindness so far, but the personality I gauge from it tells me she is completely different from me in every possible aspect. While a smile might pass for an answer this time, I don't know how much longer it will work as my get out of jail free card since I've already smiled so much today that the corners of my mouth feel as if they've gotten a good workout.

Retail life is inhumane, I think and shudder at the fact that I've only been out on the floor for a grand total of five minutes.

"Have you ever worked a register before?" she asks me brightly, and I shake my head. "It's okay. It's real easy to learn," she promises and turns to the register, giving me a quick rundown of what each button on the register does, pressing them for added emphasis. "It might seem like a lot with me running my mouth, but once you actually start doing it, it'll come easily."

I nod.

"You're kind of quiet," she says with a laugh.

"Yeah," I say laughing too, though I don't know why. It almost feels as if I'm laughing at myself, at my own awkwardness, and in a way, I guess I am.

"Hey, look. Here comes somebody," she says to me, then to the old woman who wandered up to her register, "Good morning!"

"And to you, young'un," she replies and throws eggs and milk onto the counter along with a variety of other things.

I watch Camilla dragging the things across the scanner and typing in a few things before she hands them to me. As I bag the woman's items, I smile at her and watch as Camilla cashes out the transaction. She closes the drawer with a ringing sound and passes the woman her receipt.

"Have a great day!" Camilla says to her as she takes her bags from me.

The woman smiles again but doesn't say another word as she scuttles out of the store.

Then Camilla turns back to me. "That's about it. Any questions?"

"No," I say honestly. It really *was* easy, but there is something to be said for observing compared to doing something myself.

After two more customers, Camilla gives me a try on the register, and I realize it *wasn't* as easy as it had seemed from watching her. When this woman hands me her money, I want to stand there and organize it into a neat stack with the bills all facing the same way, but I feel two sets of eyes on me, and cringing, I shove the bills into the messy piles that Camilla has stuffed lazily into the till. I close it quickly, before I see too many details to focus on, and hand the woman her change. When she walks away, I stare down at the scanner, watching as the red line tries to read a barcode on my skin that doesn't exist.

"You did it!" Camilla says, still cheerful. The only positive that I draw from her optimism is that my pessimism must not be showing that strongly…yet.

I turn to look at her through wide eyes, struggling with my

anxiety to even move when another customer approaches the register, to which Camilla replies with a simple pat to the shoulder as if I'm a dog and we're playing a game of fetch.

"You've got this!" she says, snapping on her gum as she opens a plastic bag in preparation.

I start to ring up the customer, but my progress is slower than it had been during my first attempt, and the more aware of that fact that I become, the faster I try to go. I mess up. Camilla easily fixes the problem before the woman even notices, but it rattles my nerves, and when the woman finally puts the last of her bags in the cart and leaves, I feel as if I've climbed a mountain. I'm exhausted, and my heart pounds. A few beads of sweat sit at my temple, but I resist wiping them away for fear of drawing attention to the fact that they're there to begin with.

It isn't long before Kara finds her way to my line. She snaps her gum in the same obnoxious way that Camilla had before smiling wide enough to show all her perfect white teeth. She hands me a bottle of water, and I take it from her gratefully.

"Thank you," I say, taking a sip before I set it down on the small table beside me.

"Not a problem," Kara says then looks at Camilla.

"This is Camilla," I say to her then look at Camilla. "This is my friend, Kara."

Kara holds her hand out, long pink nails shining in the light as she waits for Camilla to return the handshake. "Make sure you take care of my girl here, okay? She means the world to me."

Camilla smiles and nods, caught off guard by the statement, and I watch the exchange in amusement. Camilla is to Kara what I am to Camilla. *Interesting.*

Kara drops the handshake, and Camilla looks away as if she's searching for some sort of escape. It's strange to me that there seems to be so much tension between the two girls. With their personalities being so similar, I would assume they would click instantly. *Maybe that's the problem.*

"Hey, girl. I got your heart attack for you," Kara says to me, wiggling her eyebrows as she leans close to me.

I draw my eyebrows together before Kara gestures with her eyes for me to turn around. Inside, I wonder if I really want to do that or not, but then I see the wicked smile on her face and decide it'll be better to obey her wishes willingly. I glance over my shoulder to the opposite register, whose cashier I had neglected to acknowledge up to this point, and see a boy with black hair and brown eyes. He looks up from the item he's scanning to smile at his customer, and my knees immediately go weak.

Kara certainly knows my type, and I hate her for it.

Camilla, who I had all but forgotten about in the moment, reaches up to stifle a giggle that sounds very cartoonish. "That's Blaine," she informs us. "He's sort of…mysterious."

With my brain still in the process of trying to restore itself, I nod stupidly.

"Mysterious how?" Kara asks, not taking her eyes off him.

I risk another glance at him from the corner of my eye, but he isn't looking in our direction. I doubt he hasn't noticed three girls staring at him, and I commend him on his self-composure for not even so much as *glancing* in this direction.

"Keeps to himself," Camilla says and shrugs.

The words and gesture give me an odd look into her relationship with Blaine. I sense rejection on her, and that certainly works to heighten the 'mysterious' title he's been given. Apparently, he isn't swayed by just looks. A weird surge of hope rises in me at that.

"I know someone else like that," Kara says and pokes me in the ribs with her long fingernail. I only smile as I ring up her drink.

"Are you going to talk to him?" Kara asks, and even Camilla looks interested.

I want the floor to open up and swallow me whole. Feeling as I have a spotlight on me, I forget how to speak and look down at my shoes. If there's one thing I hate, it's being the center of attention.

I count out her change as slowly as I can to keep avoiding their looks with the hopes that they'll come up with a different topic of conversation. When I hand Kara her change, however, that wild grin is back, and I know that whatever she's about to do, I won't like.

"Blaine!" she calls out then bolts from my line as if her pants are on fire.

Camilla breaks down into laughter when he glances up from wiping down the belt on his register, but his chocolate eyes look right past her to focus on me. When our eyes meet, I can't pull mine away for all my trying, and I feel even stupider than I did the first time I had seen him. At this point, I've lost all control of my body as I stare at him.

"You're drooling," Camilla whispers in my ear.

My eyes stretch wide, and I look down to hide my face, reaching up to wipe my chin—in case I really *am* drooling—and when I look up again, I realize he's approaching. Without the tiny walls of the register blocking half of him from sight, I see how tall and fit he really is. He strides over to us, feet barely making a sound.

"New girl, huh?" he asks with a throaty chuckle and hangs his arm over the register divider.

Up close, his face is even more transfixing. His brown eyes are layered into honey and chocolate, and they sit in the perfect place within his thin, sculpted face. I nod, not wanting the terrible sound of my voice to interfere with the beautiful sound of his laughter. Still smiling, his gaze sweeps from my face downward and he reaches his long fingers toward me. His fingers brush my shirt as he lifts my nametag, bending forward to read my name in a tone slightly louder than a whisper.

"Well, Erica, I'm Blaine." He looks at Camilla then back at me. "But I'm sure you already knew that."

Again, I nod like an obedient puppy and he smiles again. "I look forward to working with you," he says and saunters back to his register to greet the elderly customer who had wandered up in his time away.

As soon as he's gone, I turn to Camilla, expecting some type of scathing look or eye roll at the very least. Instead, she smiles wide enough to reveal the lipstick on her teeth again, and I'm unnerved.

"Good for you, girl!" Camilla says, though I'm not sure exactly what I did to earn her praise.

5.

WHEN IT'S TIME for me to clock out, it's just me and Camilla left to close up the store. Blaine had clocked out hours ago, and I was glad for the loss of a distraction. As we get everything in order, and Greg overlooks the store before walking us out, I let myself really breathe for the first time that day. When I think back through the events of the day, I hadn't done much of anything, and yet, here I am, stressed to the max. I can't remember feeling like this after starting my last job. Everything had been so calm and easy, so normal.

I walk with careful, deliberate footsteps across the icy parking lot and hold onto my car for added support as I dig out the right key.

When I open the door, I see a rose on my seat along with a folded-up note. Furrowing my brow, I pick it up and open it, recognizing Kara's loopy handwriting instantly.

Great job, girl, it reads.

That puts a smile on my face as I move the flower to the passenger seat and force myself to take calm, even breaths as I get behind the wheel and begin the drive home. I did it. I made it through my first day, completely intact. And now that I know what to expect, my next day of work will come much easier…as far as my OCD is concerned, anyway.

As I pull into my driveaway, I think of possible icy patches that could be waiting as soon as I leave the comforts of my car, and that doesn't help either. So, I waddle to the door like a penguin, and when I get inside, I plop down on the couch and let myself relax…for fifteen seconds anyway. Then, I'm mad at myself again.

There's a trail of muddy water leading all the way up to me from the door. Cringing, I peel off my shoes and throw them onto my rubber doormat before I go to work cleaning up the mess I hadn't thought to avoid in the first place. When I put the mop away, I pass my room and catch a glimpse of my tote bag sitting in the shadows on my dresser.

The thought of its presence brings me some comfort. Once a week, I take an art class in the building next door to the church that houses my support group. My favorite coffee shop is right across the street from them both as if that block is dedicated to my mental well-being. Life's funny like that, but the art class is my ultimate stress relief, the one thing I can count on to make me feel better, and it's strange. From week to week, I never know what I'll be learning. In any other situation, I would be on edge, but in this one? It feels right to be able to sit back and let someone else take the wheel for a little while.

I change out of the carefully pressed outfit that I had forgotten was uncomfortable after being in it all day. Being free from the confines of the outfit, I hurry to pull on a pair of leggings under a baggy gray dress and top that off with a blue jacket. I tidy up the house—when in Rome, right—then push my way out the door, tote bag over my shoulder and hair clip firmly in place somewhere in my ginger tangles.

I toss my bag onto the passenger seat as I climb into my car, and as I drive, it jiggles precariously with each bump I go over, but I'm not worried about its contents the way I am my purse. Surprisingly, my art tote is the only thing that I can stand to let be unorganized, the only thing that can do as it pleases, and I won't feel compelled to check thrice times over. I think it has something to do with the fact that I consider this entire experience out of my control, right down to my supplies.

Ah, a hit of normalcy. It's almost addicting.

The thought causes me to smirk as I pull into the parking lot. Sniffing the air, I glance at the doors of the church next door and climb out of my car, slinging the bag over my shoulder again before I assimilate into familiar surroundings after my long day of being in new, unfamiliar places that make me feel uncomfortable in my own skin.

I push into the building, through the empty front room and down the nearest corridor. During the day, there are a lot of classes here—I can tell by the number of teachers and room numbers listed on the walls—but in the evening, there is only this one class. As I round the corner into the classroom, my teacher, Viola, smiles at me. I don't hesitate to smile back as I take my usual seat at the front of the room. After a day full of uncertain grins, it feels good to actually be smiling for *real.*

"Good to see you, Erica," Viola greets. "You seem radiant today."

"Oh, it's just the cold," I say and look down at my desk, though even beyond the stinging redness of my cheeks, I can feel the warmth from true happiness.

Viola smiles too, and I scoop up the paintbrush she places in front of me, studying the blank canvases as Viola sets them up. I stare at the beautiful array of paints on the middle of my table with a bemused expression.

This should be fun.

***

THAT NIGHT, I'M happy to relax. After the day I've had, I'm buzzing on a mixture of endorphins and the start of a caffeine crash. My day hadn't been particularly long, but it had seemed so eventful.

To think I get to do it all again tomorrow…minus the art class, of course.

I sigh wistfully, remembering Camilla and Blaine's oddness during the shift earlier and wonder if things'll always be that weird, or if that was just a one-time ordeal. I cuddle my pillow to my chest, staring up at the painting of rainbows hanging in the exact middle of the wall that divides my kitchen and living room from my place on the couch. It's pretty, in its own way. Something about the brown I had used for the mountain in the background makes me think of the brown in Blaine's eyes, and I feel like such a creep just for having the thought. I don't know him from Adam. Yet, he's on my mind at almost eleven in the evening. It's strange to be so smitten and for a stranger no less; it's a feeling I haven't had since high school.

I can't bring myself to get up, to drag myself to bed and lay down below the annoyingly low light and stare up at the perfectly angular shadows of my ceiling. After my rough day, the couch feels like Heaven. Somehow, in the poison of my own mind, I manage to fall asleep, and when I wake up, it's with all the usual obsessions and the new one in the back of my brain.

I groan and swipe a hand over my face, but for all my denial, I'm *excited* for work—a feeling I'm not used to. Of course, the anxiety is still there, but it's eased considerably from the level it was at yesterday.

I cross the house to my bathroom, arranging my makeup as carefully on my face—eyes first—as I do on the counter after I'm finished with it. I think of curling my hair but stop, realizing how ridiculous I am. Letting Kara pick me out some clothes that aren't like me is one thing but dressing up? That's a step too far. Blaine doesn't know me, and I don't know him…so why am I pampering myself like I'm about to be escorted to a fairytale ball?

Erica, you are a silly, silly girl, I chastise.

With another groan, I grab my hand towel and vigorously wash every ounce of makeup off my skin, going for a much simpler look when I reapply it. But of course, that doesn't sit right on my skin, and I scrub it off, adding more stains to the towel, and take my final approach. Satisfied, I study the creamy smears of discarded makeup on the fabric in my hands and consider tossing it into the trash can, but I can't bring myself to do it. So, instead, I throw it into the immaculately clean laundry basket beside me. I frown at the way it interrupts the perfect clean, but I force myself away. My thoughts stray to it again, but as I walk out of the bathroom, I convince myself that nothing can bring me down today.

I don't understand this newfound excitement, but no matter what, the voice in my head says, I know it doesn't have to do with my new job…more like my new chocolate-eyed coworker that's got me feeling this way. This giddiness? I recognize it only from the times I've seen Kara wear it.

Why am I so awkward? I groan to my flats as I pull them on and rush out the door.

When I pull into the parking lot, I clench and unclench my hands around the steering wheel. I'm ready and not ready. I spend a minute looking for Kara, hoping she'll have the foresight to come see me again, *knowing* how much I'll need her today. Even if she's over the top sometimes, she's also a wonderful ice breaker. Unfortunately for me, today I'm alone. I prolong making the walk inside by sitting in my car, struggling to tie my apron without the prying eyes of an audience. Uniform in place and all the time I could afford to waste spent, I make my way inside, heart lurching as I seek out Blaine. Upon not seeing him, that hope deflates with a sickening pop that I hear inside my mind.

Camilla is here and lets out a squeal when she catches sight of me. "Hey, girl! It's you and me bright and early again today."

I manage a nod, but with the lingering disappointment, it's hard to get out a coherent response. *Why do I feel like this?* I ask myself, carefully trying to make sense of my own head. *He's a stranger, and yet I'm disappointed that…what? I won't get to stare at him?*

"Looking forward to today?" Camilla asks, smile bright and hopeful again.

Another nod as I fight through my biting thoughts to appear semi-normal. My lack of actual words doesn't seem to bother her a bit. She's like a puppy, rambunctious and full of energy even if the situation around her doesn't call for it.

"So, today we're pretty slow. Sundays are usually like that…you know, church and all," she says with a lackadaisical glance around us.

"Seems about right," I say, pretending that I'm looking around at the lack of customers as well when really, I'm just using the excuse to see the empty register a few feet away.

"When it's really slow like this, they want us to pass the time by focusing on making the front of the store look good, you know, putting things back in line and just making it look pretty."

"I'm aware of the concept," I reply, and only after the words are out do I realize how snippy they really are. I don't want to be mean to Camilla, but there's something about her unwavering lightheartedness that gets to me.

She sniffles and cocks her head back a bit as if she expects me to flat out insult her.

"I'm sorry," I say quickly, looking down at my feet. Even if Camilla and Kara seem to not like one another, Camilla hasn't done a thing to me to make me feel any resentment for her. Looking into her big blue eyes leaves me feeling instantly guilty for taking a tone with her.

"You work on the lighters, I hate them," Camilla says, snapping her gum in a gesture to a plastic strip hanging off the side of the cooler. Her tone immediately tells me that's her way of getting back at me for the attitude. Not to mention how she sidestepped my entire attempt to apologize.

I shrug, not taking it to heart. If she really does have the personality of a puppy, she'll be over her feelings in a few minutes. Camilla goes to work on organizing the tiny bags of chips on the other side of the store, and I give her a passing glance as I approach the spot she had gestured to. When I actually catch sight of the lighters themselves, I bite my lip, barely resisting the urge to reach out and smack down the entire thing and stomp it until they're all so broken they'll have no other future than the trash can. Somehow, I manage to keep it together long enough to not destroy anything, instead opting to put my energy into rearranging the lighters by color and have them all face the same way. My brain feels fully engaged in the activity as I work, and once I finish, I step back to admire my work with the slightest hint of a smile on my face.

"Isn't that funny? I arrange them the same way," a voice says from behind me.

I freeze instantly, the sound of the lilting voice causing all logic in my body to shut down. Blush lining my cheeks, I turn to face Blaine and let out an awkward chuckle that I hope can come off as cute under the current circumstance. I want to say something clever, but my mind goes blank, focusing on the fact that it isn't cute when it comes down to the fact that I *have* to do things in my own way.

"H-Hi," I stutter out.

"Greetings," he says, tipping his black hat toward me, and that's when I realize he isn't dressed in a work uniform. He's wearing street clothes—jeans with a black jacket and black hat. With the shadow over his eyes, I'm once again reminded of Camilla's words—*He's mysterious.* He glances up at the clock on the wall and begins to walk deeper into the store. "I'll see you in a minute."

"O-okay," I say.

And I'm glad when he rounds the corner of the first aisle and disappears from my sight. I use the opportunity to collapse to my knees and organize the lighters all over again, waiting for the anxious tremors to go away. Just as I push the last lighter into place, I hear footsteps and look up to see Blaine again, only this time he's cloaked in his work uniform rather than street clothes. The hat is gone, revealing messy black locks.

He casts a quick glance across the aisle to where Camilla's blonde hair is visible among the chips before looking at me once more. "Are you training with her again today?"

I blink up at him, the thought of spending the day with him paralyzing. "As far as I know, yeah."

He tips his head to the side and grins. "That's too bad. It's lonely on this side of the store," he says and glances at the register beside us.

"It's lonely over there too," I say honestly, thinking of the lack of real connection between me and Camilla.

Blaine's eyes light with humor, and I smack a hand over my mouth as I realize I said that *out loud.* He leans closer to me and whispers, "We'll both survive somehow."

"Some way," I reply.

He smiles again and walks to his register. "I gotta get things set up," he says, though I'm unsure if it's to me, to Camilla, or to himself.

"Oh yeah, cool," I say in the off chance it *was* to me.

He doesn't reply, and my cheeks burn at the thought that he *wasn't* talking to me after all. *Nothing cool about that,* I chastise myself.

Camilla catches my eye across the store and gestures me back over to her register. I don't look at Blaine as I approach her. She smiles, eyes volleying between me and him. "What did he say to you?" she asks.

I shrug. "Nothing really. Just complimented me on the lighters."

She narrows her eyes, trying to better see the rack of lighters, or I assume she is anyway. Just then a customer begins to approach, and she turns her attention back to me. "You did a good job. Let's go through a quick refresher of how to run the register again."

I'm quiet as I help her bag, listening as she retells me the exact same information she had already shoved down my throat yesterday, and before I know it, half the shift has passed. Glancing over my shoulder at Blaine every few minutes gains no results, and I feel on the verge of crying out for how pathetic the whole thing is. I know that a logical person would *talk* to someone they were potentially interested in, but I know that even if I did, it wouldn't amount to anything when he found out how I really am. Yet, even with those thoughts in my head, I can't stop myself from periodically checking to see if he's looking at me.

This time, my eyes scan across the lighter display, and even from the other side of the front end, I can see that just one lighter is out of place—upside down so that its bottom lines up with the tops of the others. Cursing under my breath, I leave the comfort of the register's tiny box to fix it.

"Hey, don't worry about it. It's fine!" Camilla calls out, but it's not.

I don't know how to explain that it isn't fine if it's not perfect. I can't explain to her the way it makes me feel to see just this *one* lighter's defiance. I hear the beeping as she goes to work, scanning her next customer's items, and I take the opportunity to fix the display. I turn on my heels, ready to call an apology to Camilla now that my compulsions have been subdued when I catch sight of Blaine snickering wickedly at my little display of OCD at its finest.

6.

FRUSTRATION WELLS IN me, and I want to *cry* as I back away from the thing of lighters, but somehow, I don't. I just stand there, watching him laugh and trying to not let the moment cut me down completely. No part of this is funny, and I try to be rational—maybe he isn't even laughing at me at all and just has the worst timing in the world—but I'm paranoid and take offense to it anyway. Using my hair to shadow my face, I turn away from him and pad back over to Camilla. Thankfully, she had been too wrapped up with her customer to notice the latest interaction between me and Blaine.

I choose to say nothing and eagerly get on the register the next time she offers. It's an escape from the pain in myself, at least for a little while, and after the encounter, I found that I'm not sneaking glances at him. I'm just trying to make it through the day. An hour later, I get to clock out, grateful that I wasn't scheduled to close like I had been yesterday. I take off the apron and put on my jacket, dashing out the door without a single goodbye to Camilla or Blaine.

I hurry to my car and sit in the driver seat, staring at my red-rimmed eyes in the rearview mirror. It's a miracle that no one called me out on it. With shuddering breath, I feel the hurt all the way home, and I wish I could make it disappear. I drive the long way home, through the block where all my favorite comforts lie and stare at the church as I pass.

There are times where I desperately long for support group, when I *need* be surrounded by like-minded people, but luck is never in my favor. I pull into the parking lot and pull out my cell phone, staring at Destiny's number in particular. She encourages all of us to call at any time of the day if we need her, and I do, but I can't bring myself to push the call button. *I'm supposed to be strong,* I think and glance at the passenger seat where Kara's rose and note are still sitting.

Calling Destiny feels like I'm turning my back on all the work I've put into myself since getting the interview for this job. I compose myself and tuck my cell phone away, starting my car back up to drive the rest of the way home. I hurry inside, turning on the tea pot, and drag myself to my kitchen table. I plop down with my sketchbook and box of colored pencils, coloring carefully to recreate the rainbows in my painting, but I fail.

Sighing, I get up to get a scalding cup of tea. The pain of the liquid scorching down my throat is welcome as I sit down and attempt to draw again. All that comes out are the clouds in my mind.

***

I GO TO bed a lot sooner than I typically would, and when I wake up, I almost think it's the middle of the night still because it's so dark inside my house. A crack in the blinds of my window shows the snowstorm raging outside and for a moment, the thought makes me smile. At least the clouds aren't just in my head anymore.

The depression from the previous day is at the front of my mind as soon as I open my eyes to stare at my perfectly-centered light and a tiny voice scolds me. Why am I doing this? Locking myself away and letting the pain get to me? I'm letting myself *drown* in self-pity, I know that, but all I can think about is how I'll never be normal. I know part of me just wants to hear that I'm wrong, that eventually, I'll be able to get over my issues, that I can get through my ridiculousness and others can too.

I need someone to tell me that there's nothing wrong with me, but I doubt that even hearing those exact words would help me much in this mood. I would probably assume the speaker to be using sarcasm.

I'm trapped in my own mind.

I want to see Kara today, but I'm glad for the storm, glad that we won't be doing anything outside—Kara would have to be mental to still want to do anything of the sort—but if I know her well enough, and unfortunately, I do, she *is* that crazy. I roll over and check my phone, no calls or texts, but that's nothing new. Before I even get out of bed, I call her.

"What's the game plan?" I ask as soon as she answers.

"No stroll around the park," she resolves, and I hear the pout. "No, instead we're gonna hit the town."

"Really?" I ask, chuckling, and I'm glad she had a plan B in check. Never before have I craved friendship so strongly. "Hopefully somewhere with lots of alcohol."

Now it's Kara's turn to laugh. "Cheers to that. Get dressed, and we'll still have an awesome day, you'll see."

Despite not really wanting to go out when I can stay here and sleep, I force myself to get up and do exactly as she says. If I let myself listen to the voice in my head, it will continually drag me down. I've learned from experience it's better to listen to Kara, and besides, it'll be good for me to be distracted from myself for a while. If Kara is good at anything, it's bringing life to the dead.

Kara reaches my house just as I finish putting my face together, even though she lives on the other side of town, and I'm impressed. She can be a real speed demon when she wants to be. I rush to open the door, and Kara appears bright and sparkly and well…Kara. She's wearing another pink shirt, this one covered with a glittery, sparkling butterfly. I've always preferred moths to butterflies. They aren't flashy or cocky; they mind their own business and just try to blend in with their surroundings and live their lives. They don't want to be seen, and that's something I can relate to.

I am the moth to Kara's butterfly.

"Surely that's not what you're wearing!" she exclaims, putting her hands on her hips as she frowns at my pajamas.

I shake my head. "Of course not. I haven't had a chance to get dressed yet."

"Wonderful," she says and hands me a bag. "Here you go."

I blink, tilting my head to the side. "*More* clothes?"

Her eyes brighten. "Yes, more clothes!"

"How much does that bring my total up to now? One hundred dollars? Two?"

She waves her hand. "Zero. Now go try it on."

I want to argue, but I also don't want her to start trying to dress me herself, so I turn to go the bathroom before I open the bag and see what she's brought me today. I'm relieved to see a pair of jeans, a simple white shirt, and a plaid button down top. These *are* my style. I clutch them tight to my chest, feeling the tears bubble in the corners of my eyes.

It's as if she could tell how much I needed a friend. I put the clothes on, feeling them hug my skin, and take them off to straighten them before pulling them back onto my body. I take them off for the last time and straighten out a few remaining bulges before pulling them on again and going out to the living room to where Kara is waiting.

She stands up, smiling as she catches sight of me. "Do a turn so I can see *all* of it."

I obey and spin slowly.

Kara gives me a thumbs up, and I feel my hardened face melt into a smile. I'm so grateful to have her, someone to sympathize with me, who *knows* I'm not right but loves me anyway. She protects me and goes out of her way for me like the sister I never had.

We climb into her car, and I stare at her, waiting for her to clue me in on the plan for today.

"I'm thinking tequila and Mexican food," she replies.

I tilt my head to the side. "It's noon."

"That means nothing to me," she says calmly though there's a crazy smile on her face as she starts the engine.

I smile back and relax against my seat. "Yes, ma'am. You're the boss."

"So glad you agree. It would've been lame if I would've had to kidnap my best friend."

"Nope. I'm fully yours to take," I reply, and she speeds off.

I grip into the chair like I'm on a rollercoaster ride. She's the only person I know who can floor it in a residential neighborhood and never get pulled over. All my reservations, I keep to myself.

She's true to her word about it still being a good day. We go out to eat, have some drinks, and laugh. For just a while, I forget about who I am and my issues…until Kara decides she needs to pick something up from my newest place of employment, and the entire scene from the day before crashes down on me once again.

Sitting in the parking lot, I can nearly *hear* Blaine's laughter in the back of my head. Kara smiles at me, oblivious. She has no idea about yesterday's incident because I had made sure to not tell her. Sometimes, I feel it makes our friendship easier to maintain when I hold onto stories about my episodes…especially when those stories involve boys.

"Come on," Kara urges me out of the car, and despite my thoughts, I follow her inside the store with my eyes squeezed shut.

I am a glutton for punishment.

Kara says nothing as we walk by the registers, but she doesn't have to. I can tell by how slowly she walks that he's here, and I peek just long enough to confirm I'm right. Camilla is here too, but I doubt Kara has even taken notice of her.

My best friend is in the lead as we finally turn down an aisle, putting the registers out of view. She maneuvers through the store until we find the snack aisle. Wobbling slightly with the tipsy effect of our drinks, she grabs an armful of chips and looks at me with a frown. When she sees the basket dangling from my fingertips, her face mashes into a smile. I already know she didn't have things planned out this far ahead.

Maybe she's drunker than I thought.

"Geez, think that'll be enough?" I say with a laugh as I feel the weight of the basket increase drastically.

"You never know," she says, and we make our way back to the front.

Kara is again in the lead and picks a line before I can protest, so I don't. It's Blaine's line, if I know Kara, so I try to distract myself from the upcoming encounter by looking at the covers of the magazines in the rack beside us, trying without success to convince myself that it doesn't matter who's line we're actually in.

What if he laughs at you again? a tiny voice asks.

He has nothing to laugh at, I inform it.

Didn't stop him before.

I grit my teeth, unable to think of a rational thought to combat that one.

"What does that even mean…*King's* size?" Kara's voice cuts into my head as she scoffs, tossing down a candy bar on the shelf with a thump.

It's almost as if I can hear it *scream* when it lands in a place clearly not meant for it. Frowning, I snatch it up and rush to put it back in place, eyes on Kara the entire time.

Kara laughs, and I flinch at the sound, mentally comparing it to Blaine's. "You're something else, girl…you know that?"

Most of the time, she knows better than to do something like that when she's with me, but there are also times when she does it on purpose to push me to the limit. I wonder which of the two options this incident happens to fall under. I shrug and look away, not wanting to feel hurt, but I do anyway. That's one way to say it, I suppose. My eyes catch sight of the lighter display at the end of the magazine rack, and although they are arranged in the right color order, the tops face the opposite way than I prefer, and I feel that wiggle of discomfort in the pit of my stomach again.

"Speaking of something else," Kara says, waggling her eyebrows as we near the front of the line, but I'm only half paying attention. I already guessed it was Blaine's line, that she set me up again, but it's fine because all I can focus on are the lighters.

"Give me the basket," she urges, and I realize Blaine's waiting on us.

When my eyes meet his, he smiles at me. "Hello, Erica."

"I thought you said you organize them the same way as me," I accuse and slam the basket onto the conveyer belt, laying into him without bothering to return his hello.

"I do," he says, small smile on his face that I can tell comes from surprise as he begins to take each item out. Instead of scanning them as he picks them out, he sets them in various piles around his register. "Just with my own flair to it."

I shake my head, ruffling my hair and glare at the display over my shoulder as he begins to scan the items. It's like I can *hear* the lighters calling out to me, mocking me even. "This will never do," I say, stomping over to the rack to forcefully shove the lighters back into place. The beeping sounds of scanning stop as he pauses to watch me, and I wonder if he'll laugh again.

"Girl, really?" Kara asks, raising her eyebrows before her eyes gesture to Blaine.

I've gotten really good at reading Kara's face over the years. and I know what that expression means. It's disappointment. Here she is trying to find me a perfect boyfriend, yet I can't keep my neuroses in check long enough to keep them from running away. I can't bring myself to care. If a guy runs from something as small as *this*, they are in no way, shape, or form able to handle me anyway.

"You know you don't *have* to work today, right?" Blaine asks, tapping his fingers on his register as he scans the last item.

I only acknowledge him after the work is done. "Ta-da," I say, gesturing to it with a sideways look to Blaine. "This is the way they should be."

Blaine smiles, and I wait for the laugh, surprised when it doesn't come. His eyes are sparkling in amusement, but there's no bad feeling in my gut to accompany it.

Brain, what does this mean?

Kara shakes her head and pays. "I apologize for my friend," she says but doesn't meet my eyes as the words leave her lips. It's like she's suddenly embarrassed to be seen out in public with me.

"Nothing to apologize for," Blaine assures her then to me, "Well, I'll see you later." Then, he's onto the next customer in his line.

Kara is icily silent as we walk to the door but as soon as we make it to the parking lot, she asks, "What just happened?"

I look at her, waiting for her to continue. I have no idea which social boundary I've breached this time, but I'm sure she's more than happy to tell me. I can nearly *feel* my insides shriveling in disappointment at her tone. The day has been *wonderful* up to this point…so how had it come to this?

"You have a hot guy trying to talk to you, and you practically blow him off for some lighters?" Her words don't hurt as much as her overall skepticism does.

I stiffen at the venom in her tone—she may be my best friend, but she doesn't get me. She's never gone to support group—never had to—but ultimately, I wish she would take it upon herself as my best friend to do so, at least once. Just so she could see that there are others like me, that I don't *choose* to be like this. She's never said it out loud, but I know that part of her thinks I can just get over my compulsions if I really try, but I know from experience that I can't. I'm a broken person, maybe unfixable. Sometimes, I think about it from her point of view, and I can't really blame her for getting upset. It must be a bummer to have a bubbly personality like she does but a rock of a friend like me always around to constantly weigh her down.

A lot of times, I wonder why she's put up with me for all the years that she has when it would be so much easier for her to walk away and pretend she never knew me.

"I don't expect you to understand," I say at last.

"Good, because I don't," she says bitterly

I shrug in response. I've definitely been told worse.

7.

THE FIGHT WITH Kara is so stupid, so *passive,* and yet, I still don't talk to her for the rest of the day. She drops me off at home with a less than stellar goodbye, and I trudge inside, staring at my muddy shoes. This time, I take them off on the rubber mat, staring at my rainbow painting on the wall. I hate it today and consider tearing it down, tossing it right out into the snow to rot, but I know that without it, the wall will look too bare.

I strip off my clothes, not even bothering to put on pajamas. I crawl into bed in just my underclothes and clutch my pillow, letting it soak up the tears that find their way free every few minutes. After our argument, my self-hatred is unnaturally strong ,and I wish I could fall asleep just to have a couple of hours where I won't have to think about it. Instead, I lay in the darkness of my room, phone beside my head.

I pick it up and squint against the light as I read the screen. There's no messages, but I hadn't expected there to be. With a groan, I toss my phone to the floor and get up. I go to the bathroom and pull out my bottle of sleeping pills from the cabinet. I stare at the bottle for a long moment with a sigh. If there's one thing I hate, it's taking these. It's not natural, but every once in a while, like today, I find that I have no other choice. I pop one of the pills into my mouth and swallow it down along with all of my reservations. As soon as my head hits the pillow, I'm asleep.

WHEN MY EYES open again a few hours later, I feel hungover. Clamping my hand over my mouth, I rush to the toilet and throw up a mouthful of stomach acid. Grimacing at the taste, I move to the sink and rinse my mouth out with three handfuls of water. I stare at my reflection, finding no humor in it today, and decide that just washing my face isn't going to cut it today. I jump into the shower and scrub my skin until its red and raw. As I climb out, I wrap a towel around myself and frown. Usually, I feel renewed after a good shower, but the surge of emotions from yesterday is still there, just as strong as the day before that, and the day before that. I'm eventually going to have to come to terms with the fact that it's just a new addition to my routine.

Feeling upside down about my job, my friend, and *myself,* I throw on one of my old outfits, finding it too difficult to put on one that Kara picked out, and make a pot of coffee, tapping my nail eagerly on the counter. I want to believe that today will bring me something good, but I can't imagine what. I drink three cups of coffee, despite my brain warning me that that might not be the best idea but somehow, I'm still tired. It's like I have a leak in my skin where all my energy seeps away just as soon as I create it.

I drive exceptionally slow, still feeling the aftereffects of the sleeping pill. The only remarkable thing about my hangover is that I don't stew in my car, thinking about my anxiety. Instead, I climb out of the car, and when I finally make it inside, I see Blaine is at the first register. My eyes catch his before I even realize he's what I'm seeing.

"Hi!" he calls cheerfully, looking up from counting the money in his drawer.

I stutter a pathetic, "Hello" in response as I shuffle past to get my own till for the opposite register. I count out the money in triple sets of threes just to make sure it's right. My head is pounding so badly that I would believe two plus three equals six. When I get the money counted, I shuffle over to my register and get that prepped as well. I look around, expecting to see Camilla's bright blonde hair at any moment, but I don't see it.

It must be her day off.

Me and Blaine, alone. I swallow roughly and glance at him from the corner of my eye, but he's engaged in a conversation with an elderly woman, and thankfully, he doesn't notice. I try not to focus on that thought. I take a sip off my water bottle then work on pulling a few customers out of Blaine's line. I throw myself into my job today, trying to not let my headache shut me down completely.

As I count out a customer's change, I see him looking at me from the corner of my eye. *He's trying to talk to you, and all you care about are some lighters?* I can nearly *hear* Kara's singsong scolding in my head.

I think about tearing a chunk of my hair out just to have something else to think about. Thankfully, Mondays prove to be busier than Sundays had been. When a break in customers comes, I actually dread it, ringing up my last customer in line as slowly as I can manage because I know that once I'm alone with my thoughts, they'll torture me all over again. I watch my hands work but from the corner of my eye, I still see him.

Blaine wipes down the belt on his register before glancing around his side of the store and sauntering over to me. "Just you and me today?" he asks, leaning his arms on the divider to peer down at me.

My heart beats in my chest as I finish counting out the customer's change. "Uh-huh," I reply, hoping my face isn't as red as I imagine it to be.

He smiles and leans down a bit. That's when I realize his gaze is trained on my open drawer. "So, it's been you...*you're* the one leaving the immaculate drawers in their wake?"

I duck my head to hide the blush and look at the offending item in question. "Guilty as charged."

He leans closer to me, so close that I can smell his spearmint gum, and I just stare at his lips, imagining what it would be like to kiss him. Time seems to freeze as we stand there, looking at one another.

"I do the same," he admits at last.

I perk up at the confession and close my drawer to pass the lady her money. "Yeah?"

He nods and wipes at the corner of his mouth. "Yeah." He chuckles. "I also have to make sure they all face the same way when I give someone back their change."

"Really?"

He nods and pulls his face tight. "Wait. You're not going to laugh?"

My brows furrow instantly. "Why would I laugh?" I ask, trying not to think again of the way he had laughed at me.

"Camilla did…the first time she noticed me doing that."

"She said you were strange," I tell him.

He laughs and reaches up to scratch the back of his neck. "That's one word for it, I suppose. My doctor calls it obsessive compulsive disorder."

I turn toward him, staring at him with such a mix of emotions that I wonder if I've lost the rest of my mind. He's…like me? Is it possible the chuckle from the other day hadn't come from malice but *understanding* like some kind of inside joke that only people with compulsions get? This development makes things so much more interesting. The thing I hide the most about myself now seems to be my ticket for starting a conversation with Blaine.

But how?

"A lot of people don't understand," he says, smile dropping off his face and just like that, he seems like someone else—*vulnerable* even. "That's why I tend to keep to myself."

There's a statement I can relate to, I think, remembering back to my conversation with Kara. "They really don't."

The smile returns on his face, a ghost of its former self, before he pats the divider with each hand. "Customer," he says apologetically and goes back to his own register to help them.

"Talk to you later," I call after him, surprising myself with the sentence.

The rest of the day seems to go in that fashion. We say a line or two every few hours, working hard for the time in between. With about an hour left until the end of my shift, the crowd dies down, and we're left to clean up the front of the store. There are chips and magazines tilted and tossed everywhere, and my compulsions are twisting so deeply inside of me that I fear I might throw up despite my hangover having worn off hours ago.

Blaine goes to work around his register, straightening the bags of chips on the tiny aisle by him. For me, the chips are easy to ignore. It's the lighters that draw my attention. They've been left in such a disorganized fashion that I can't even think of them without picking at my skin for a distraction.

With a strangled sound climbing up my throat, I push myself onward and knock all of them off of the display. Scattered on the floor, they make me uneasy as well, but it's better than the feeling they left me with a moment ago. I crouch down onto my knees and one-by-one, I put them back in the perfect order. My chest swells in pride when it's done, and the little voice inside congratulates me on a job well done.

I turn my attention to helping Blaine with the chips. He smiles at me when the sound of my sneakers squeaking on the floor announces my arrival.

"Come to help?" he asks.

"If you *need* my help."

"Of course. You take this shelf, and I'll work on the one over here," he decides.

I agree, and he moves to his aisle as I stare at the portion of chips I've been assigned, trying to find the best way to go about my newest task at hand. Chips are easier to organize than the lighters had been, and when I've finished, I move to head back to my register. Then I stop, a cold chill creeping down my spine when my eyes catch sight of the lighter display, and I cringe—they're flipped around in the opposite direction of the way that they need to be.

I huff and rush over to them, hearing a blast of laughter from farther down the aisle, the same laughter that had made me crumple in on myself the other day. I turn to see Blaine with a huge smile on his face, laughter pouring from his mouth, and suddenly my brain figures out what just happened—he's *playing* with me. That's what he had done the first time too, right? He never meant to hurt my feelings.

You are *a very silly girl,* I think to myself coldly. How could I have misjudged him so severely?

"You *moved* them!" I accuse, eyes stretched wide as I move them into the exact same pattern I had done ten minutes prior.

"Oh, why oh why, can't your brain be wired the same way as mine? It's like we're competing in the OCD games or something,"

Blaine jokes, walking over to me with his arms folded over his chest.

I'm not used to hearing the abbreviation out loud. Usually, Destiny and the other members of support group shorten it to 'compulsions' or on a good day, urges. They never say the term as if they think denial is the first step to recovery, though I have to admit that I hate the name of it too.

"You're determined!" he tacks on, studying my profile.

I laugh, and as the sound comes from my lips, I realize how natural it *feels*. It's so nice to laugh. "They say women know best," I reply, lifting my chin to eye him as soon as the last lighter is in place. Crush or no crush, my brain does *not* like his method of organization, and briefly, I consider super gluing the lighters just to keep him from moving them again.

I hear the muffled sound of his voice as he says something to me, but I can't focus on him like a normal girl could. *God, when did I become jealous of Kara?*

He lifts his hand, and it draws my attention. I narrow my eyes, assuming he's about to mess up all of my hard work once again, but he doesn't. He holds both hands up, palms out and says, "You win."

"Good," I beam, chin held out as I go to work organizing the first rack of magazines by the register.

Blaine follows me, hands in his pockets, and my heart skips a beat, wondering if he's got something to tell me. And what it is if he does? "So, are the lighters and the magazines your only quirks?"

I pause—not what I had expected, but interesting all the same. I don't answer right away, and he doesn't move. It's like the entire scene has been captured with a freeze frame moment like '80's shows do to give the main character a chance to talk to the audience. The only problem here? I *have* no audience to bounce my ideas off of. However I answer him is my choice, and mine alone.

You should be honest, comes the moral part of my personality, and I want to obey but telling the truth to anyone outside of support group is something I've never tried before. *Technically, he* did *ask.* "I-I do things in threes," I say at last. He raises an eyebrow, and I take that as a sign to continue. "I wash my hands three times, I put my clothing on three times over, I lock the door three times before leaving the house…that kind of thing."

Blaine nods as if that makes perfect sense, and I have to wonder that if it *does* in his compulsively wired brain. "Mine isn't numerical. I-I'm a bit more complicated than that."

"How so?" I ask, genuinely interested to know.

He looks away, and I study his profile, the way his lips curl downward into a slight frown like he's having his own freeze-frame moment. The longer the moment drags out, the weirder it begins to feel. He might not share in the affliction at all—a lot of people make jokes about little things being OCD when they're nowhere near the same level as me. I deflate a bit at the thought. *If something seems too good to be true, it usually is.*

Or maybe he really does have it, and this moment is just as difficult for him as it had been for me. Blaine breathes in through his teeth and takes a step closer. We're so close now that our chests nearly touch, his nametag brushes my apron when he lifts a hand to wipe at his mouth, and I ignore the flutter in my heart caused by our proximity. I focus on his chocolate brown eyes with the intensity of everything hanging in the air.

"You won't think I'm weird?" he asks, face drawn tight as if this is an impossible thing he's asking for.

I shake my head and his face is right next to mine, his closeness making it difficult to remember how to breathe. "Promise?" he asks, setting his hand on mine.

"Promise." My dry throat cracks at the gesture. The touch of his skin sends electricity buzzing through me, so strong that I almost forgot the point of the promise in the first place. I might as well be a drone—I've lost all control over myself at this point anyway.

He pulls his hand away and picks at the edge of his apron as if he's suddenly too shy to make eye contact. "Mine works in checks."

"Checks?" I ask, tilting my head.

He pulls his lips tight, looking away as if doesn't know how to explain himself. "I have a number of things that have to be *perfect* before I can leave the house or go to bed or do anything really."

I blink but don't interrupt as he pulls his words together. I've heard of cases like his before, some of them from support group—his is the most severe form of OCD that I've heard of. Thankfully, I've never experienced it myself.

"If everything's not perfect, I have to start over with the routine from the beginning. Sometimes, it gets to the point where I spend hours just trying to get it right because I miss sleep and can't focus," he says, hanging his head as if he's ashamed to admit that.

The look on his face is full of pure shame, and I realize something—he's just confided in me something that he's *ashamed* of. Something that he most likely doesn't tell a lot of people. When I see that look on his face, I want to reach out and pull him into a hug but can't bring myself to do it.

"Have you ever talked to someone about it?" I ask him, hoping my tone doesn't come off as disinterested. The thought of him going to support group with me creeps into my mind, and I'm not sure what to do with the image it conjures.

His eyes move from the floor to meet mine. "I've never been to a therapist. Too embarrassing."

My heart thumps for a different reason than my hormones, and I realize that I'm *sad* for him. The prison of my own mind is the worst pain I face, and seeing others in the same position hurts *me* too.

With shaking fingers, I work up the courage to set my hand on his shoulder. He peers at me through the strands of his black hair as I say, "Don't be embarrassed! It's not as if people like us *choose* our quirks. I've never been ashamed of mine, and I know that's partly due to my mother's support and my friends from support group. It's good to be around people who understand."

"Ugh, support group," he says and lifts his hand to shield his eyes as if he's avoiding looking at something unpleasant.

"Have you ever gone to one?" I ask and pull my hand away,

wondering if I've just found a way to make him feel even worse.

He nods and looks across the store, a blank expression on his face. "Once but…it wasn't for me." He swipes his tongue across his teeth. "It really helps you?"

I shrug. "In a way. Knowing I have an outlet, other people who understand me, lifts most of the weight off of my shoulders. It's kind of what AA is to alcoholics, I guess."

Blaine bobs his head and snickers at the analogy before he looks away sharply, pretending to survey for customers even though the bell chime of the door hasn't gone off for a good thirty minutes. He's avoiding eye contact at this point, and I don't blame him.

I'm *glad* for his choice in gestures.

"I visit my group once a week. It used to be three times a week, but after my mother died, I started to depend less on others and focus more on myself. I have a website that I go to for advice and helpful exercises that push me through the harder days when I don't go to group. They're great stress relievers," I say.

"What's the name of it? I might check it out."

It should've come to me instantly, but as I stare up into his ungodly perfect face, I draw a blank. "I-I can't remember," I say at last.

Blake blinks. "Oh okay."

I want to hit myself when I hear the tone of his voice—the last thing I want is for him to think I'm *lying.*

The bell above the door dings as a group of teenagers comes in and Blaine eyes them though I can't tell if it's with unease or gratitude. He looks back at me and says, "Well, I'll tell you what. Add me online or something, and if you think of it, send me the link, and while you're at it, give me the information for your support group too."

"O-okay," I stutter.

He turns away but then glances back at me as if wants to say more but goes to his register without a word. With my personal space back, I feel more like myself, and I breathe normally again, thinking of just how odd my day has become.

8.

WHEN I DRIVE home, I picture the way Blaine had looked at me through his bangs, a combination of beauty and sadness, and for all my trying, I can't get the thought to leave my mind. When I get home, I think about looking Blaine up, but I don't want to seem too desperate or clingy. How long would a normal person wait? I try to think of Kara, but that does little to help me. She's the impulsive type—she would've done it right on the spot. I tilt my head to the side, thinking of the odd situation I've just walked into. He *confided* in me, didn't he? He's given me a skeleton directly from his closet.

I'm not sure if I would call it friendship, per se, but it has to count for something, right?

Pushing away all my reservations, I look him up anyway, wishing I can text Kara for advice, but we haven't talked since our fight. Pushing my hair from my eyes, I stare at the computer screen. Blaine's profile is easy enough to find—there's a picture of him wearing a hat and holding a beer at what looks like some type of party—and before I think it all the way through, I send him a friend request before my nerves convince me that it's a bad idea. I read through the information in his bio, and my eyes linger a bit on the relationship status—single—before I hit the message button and send the location and meeting dates of support group.

Once the message sends, I stare at the little word beneath my message. *Nothing to do now but wait.*

That seems creepy too, just sitting here, waiting for the second 'sent' turns to 'read.' Even if *he* doesn't know it, *I* do, and I don't want to be that girl. I never want to be that attached to anyone, not even Kara. I push away from the desk and look around my house, desperate for a distraction of any kind. Then I spot the red container next to my couch and realize I *must* have been out of it to have left it here. The box is full of Christmas decorations, and I've all but forgotten about it since I drug it out of the garage about a week ago.

With Christmas less than two weeks away, now is as good of a time as any to finally get decorations out of the way. With a wistful sigh, I pull my coat and gloves on and glare at the container, wishing it would put itself where I need it to be. While I might adore Christmas, I've never cared for the decorating part that comes with it. I huff and puff as I drag the box of lights outside into the snow.

With a groan, I put a hand on my lower back and stand up straight, surveying the blank face of my house. This is my first year doing this alone, and I'm not sure where or how to begin. How do you even decide? I stall for time by popping the top off and stare at the contents inside, hoping for inspiration from the source…or maybe an instruction guide. On the top of the bin are three different bunches of Christmas lights—one is rainbow, one is all blue, and the last is green and red.

Immediately, I overlook the possibility of using the red and green ones. More of the red lights are broken than the green, and it's a noticeable ratio. Even thinking of the uneven coloring leaves me wondering why I haven't just thrown the entire bundle away. It's not like I can ever bring myself to use them again.

On instinct, I go for the blue lights, not because I like them so much, but for the fact that if one or two of the lights don't work, it'll be much harder for me to notice. I work on unwinding the roll, cursing a few times under my breath as my gloves get caught in the wires. At last, I have the bundle under control and a respective amount of lights lay lazily in my hands.

I start by looping them on the railing of the porch, just over the top metal bar, and step back to see my work. Then, I frown. It's sagging in the middle, and that sickening twinge pinches my stomach. I rush to undo it, and with resolved determination, I set to restringing it, trying to make it as straight as I can possibly manage.

It sags in less places this time but it's still noticeable—on my radar, at least— and I fix it once again. Crossing my fingers, I study my efforts of the third attempt and sigh in relief that it's accomplished. My inner critic can be a real pain when she wants to be.

Mentally crossing the first step off my list, I turn to the box to see what's next and the more I stare, the worse I feel. There are two light-up deer in here. Not three and not one but two…the worst number in my opinion. If there was one, I could put it in the middle of the lawn and be done with it. Three would be even better since I could arrange them in a triangle formation, but two? What can I possibly do with that?

I *could* leave one in the box, of course, and just put one in the middle of the lawn, but the knowledge that the other one is still tucked away would very much eat at me. As I stare at them, I just want to tear my hair out. In the end, I put the two deer on each corner of the lawn, the ones closest to the street and farthest from the house. It's not the best, and I still consider going to the store to buy a third one even though I'll be stressed for money until I get my first check. As I put the lid back on the red container, I survey the deer again and find that even though I'm not happy with it, I can live with it.

That's something.

9.

WHEN THE NEXT day comes, I wake up in a less than stellar mood again. After having dragged the red container back to my garage last night, my lower back is screaming in a fresh wave of pain that makes me sick. I pop up to take some aspirin, and as I dig through the drawer in the kitchen, my eyes land on a picture of my mother that I keep hanging in the middle of the wall like a shrine.

I pause to stare at it before I pop the pill in my mouth and swallow it down without water, wincing at the bitter taste. I try not to think of my mother if I can help it. It's been less than a year since she was killed in a car accident, and I still have a lot of emotions to work through. With shaking fingers, I reach out to touch the edge of the frame and then pull my fingers back as if I'm afraid the picture will burn me.

I think of the day I have ahead. I have support group and that's it. There's time to visit her grave but I'm not sure I can manage it. *We'll see what it comes to,* I tell myself as I push through my morning routine.

You can go on the way to support group, the little voice in my head says.

I consider it since I drive past the cemetery where my mother rests nearly every day.

Only terrible daughters don't visit their mothers, the voice insists, and my insides squeeze with a painful protest before I give up. It's right. As I grab my phone off the table, I spare a glance at myself in the mirror hanging by the door. My orange hair is bundled into a messy bun on the top of my head but other than that, I look decently put together.

Well, as put together as a woman going to visit her dead mother can look.

In the back of my mind sounds the funeral dirge as I stomp to my car, wary of any potential new ice patches formed during the night, and get into my car. I pull down the visor to look at my reflection again, and wish I hadn't. All the poor sleep is really starting to catch up to me. I slam the visor shut and start to drive. The cemetery has a stone path designed to drive on, but I park my car in the street anyway and walk across the snow encrusted field.

The crunch of the white powder beneath my feet is the only sound I hear. I glance up, shielding my eyes from the sun as I try and gauge my surroundings. My mother's grave lies at the back of the field, closest to the oak tree which is visible in the distance. The sight quickens my pace, and before I know it, I'm staring at her gravestone.

I sink to my knees, not even thinking of the cold or the snow as I whisper, "Hi, Mama."

MY FACE IS red, blotchy, and frozen from crying in the cold when I climb back into my car. If I thought I had looked less than stellar before, I look like a nightmare now. It doesn't matter. Support group has seen me *through* my mother's death. There have been plenty of days in which I looked a lot worse. Besides, I don't really expect Blaine to show up. If he's as embarrassed as it seemed at the store, there's no way he'd come to talk to a bunch of strangers, right?

He finds comfort in you, the voice insists.

I sigh, wishing I could go a day without arguing against myself.

I start the engine and relax into the comfort and familiarity of my normal support group routine. Driving down the road, I adjust my mirror slightly and merge into traffic on the highway. The drive usually gives me anxiety, but today, it passes me by. It's not hard for me to guess why—my mind is in other places.

This is ridiculous, I chastise myself, patting the knot of hair on my head.

That doesn't stop the stupid thoughts, though. I take my exit and find my way into the parking lot before turning off the engine. I breathe in and out a few times which also doesn't help the thoughts and venture into the cold chill of December air once again. It hits me harder this time because the snow from the cemetery melted on my knees. I suddenly find myself glad for my choice to wear black pants.

Temporarily, the cold chills me—how high had the heater *been* exactly? My breath puffs out little white clouds as I make my way across the parking lot, teeth chattering even when I wrap my arms around myself. I stop once I reach the doors and look back over the path I've just traveled, scanning the parking lot though what I'm looking for, I have no clue.

Yes, you do, the voice says.

Normal, I say to myself, trying to tune it out. *Just act normal.* But the word has lost all meaning. So, I pretend that I'm not having an internal conflict with myself—again—as I push my way inside and sit in the usual seat beside Serena. I move to put my bag on the floor when I realize something is different…there's an *extra* chair in the room, and Blaine is perched on it.

My mouth runs dry at the sight of him, and if I thought I was ditzy before, it has nothing on this moment. "You came," I state stupidly.

"I told you I'd check it out," he says.

I open my mouth but close it again. I doubt he wants to hear that I thought he was a liar.

A small smile crosses Serena's lips as she glances at him then me then him again. She gets up, clutching her small purse in her fist.

"Oh, you don't have to get up, Serena," I say.

"I know," she replies, voice sweet as always.

As she smiles at Blaine, I understand. She wants him to feel *welcome* here and is doing her part to ensure he doesn't run away. Blaine isn't as quick to react, so Serena pats the chair she had been seated on like he's a cat. He doesn't protest as he and Serena swap seats.

Wrapping his arms around himself, he says, "It's cold in here."

"You get used to it," I say, but with the heat flushing through my face, it's impossible to imagine ever feeling cold again.

The other members of the group are engaged in their own conversation on the other side of the room, and Blaine watches them, rolling the edge of his sleeve in his fingers. "So, how does this work?"

His nervousness is so raw that it hits me the way he doesn't even *try* to hide it. He's really putting a lot of faith into this meeting, and that both makes me feel good, and scares the Hell out of me. If something happens to scare him off, he'll be against group therapy for a long time, possibly forever, and it'll be my fault. I open my mouth, but before I can say a word in reply, Destiny enters, and a wave of silence flashes through the room as we smile at her and then the greetings begin. Destiny waves back but her eyes are glued on Blaine as she plops into her chair and I can nearly *hear* the warning bells going off in her mind, the ones that react to the slightest bit of change.

"Hello there! It's been so long since we've had a new member," she says, clutching the papers in her hands a bit tighter.

"I asked him to come," I say, lifting my hand to break her concentrated stare on Blaine.

Her eyes shift to me and soften slightly at the familiarity of my face. She nods once and looks back at him. "Well, alright then. You'll be our opener today, young man. Tell us a bit about yourself."

I'm not happy for her calling out Blaine so soon, but I *am* impressed at how easily she's able to reel herself in from her internal conflict. Blaine tries to stand up and stumbles when his foot gets caught on the rung, but he recovers easily and looks around the small group with such wide eyes that I have no doubt he's regretting his decision to come. He seems so different here than at the store and it's hard to imagine that this is the same person.

"Well, my name is Blaine and uh…" He reaches up to scratch the back of his neck, eyes moving from Serena to Destiny, and finally me. I try to offer him a small smile of encouragement. He holds the look as he says, "I have compulsions so crippling that on some days, I can't even leave the house. I've never uh…talked about it to anyone, so this is really new to me."

He sits down so quickly that it's as if some invisible force shoved him backward. Alice stares at Blaine with sympathy, the most able to relate. Her compulsions have been so bad in the past that a few times, we've visited her home on support group days because she couldn't leave her house to come to us.

I don't know what urges me to do it, but I reach out and squeeze Blaine's hand encouragingly. He doesn't pull away, instead choosing to squeeze my hand back, but as soon as I catch myself still holding him, I let go quickly.

"I'm sorry to hear that," Destiny says. "But it's nice to see you here, Blaine. We're a safe place. We're all like you in some aspect, and I hope that you are able to find comfort in us on your worst days."

Blaine bobs his head, but his eyes are on his fingers.

Destiny, sensing that Blaine is on the verge of shutdown, turns to me. "Erica, how has your week been? When we left off last, you were in the middle of seeking out a new job. Any promising leads?"

I can't help looking at Blaine. "Yeah, I uh…actually got a job as a cashier at a little mom and pop store."

Blaine raises his hand, sheepish smile on his face. "Witness."

Destiny's eyes fill with amazement. "That's great! And how do you feel about it?"

"It seems…good. Different from my last job but dependable."

"Good, good, and how have you handled your stress?"

Now, it's not so easy to meet Blaine's eyes. I think of the night I spent crying on the floor after the first time he laughed at me, and I don't want to admit any of it out loud.

"Erica?" she prompts after a full minute of silence goes by.

Now you know how Blaine felt.

"It's been…*tough* but my art classes have really helped. We started painting this week. Acrylics, not watercolor."

"Excellent therapy," she encourages with a nod of approval that matches the smile on her face. "I gave it a try for a while." Her eyes scan the rest of the group as she taps her pen against her papers. "It's something I recommend you all give a try, even if you haven't gotten an artistic bone in your body."

WHEN GROUP ENDS, I try to hurry and sling my bag over my shoulder to rush out the door before Blaine can stop me, but he must've guessed I'd try something like that because he's waiting for me just outside.

"So, you're an artist?" he asks, eyes wide and twinkly like a curious kid.

I want to be dignified in my moment of shame, but one look at him dissolves that hope away. "Yeah, sometimes, I guess."

"That's cool," he says, patient grin on his face. "I've never been much of an artsy person. I can draw a mean stick figure, though."

I crack a smile at that. "I'm more into abstract work."

He bobs his head. "I might be able to get into that. Maybe I can come with you to your art class sometime."

I raise an eyebrow. "You'll be tired of me if you see me *everywhere,*" I say before I can stop myself.

He smiles. "How could I ever be bored of such an interesting girl?"

10.

I N THE BASEMENT of the church, my clothes had dried somewhat but not nearly enough to be comfortable. I'm so cold by the time I get back home that it's easy to forget about Blaine and support group. A hot bath is all that's on my mind. I set my gloves on the table and put on a pot of coffee, eager for something warm. I set a tentative finger to the side of the teapot, and the warmth surges into my frozen skin. A ding sounds from my computer and I startle at the sound, nearly tripping over my feet to see what the notification shows—Blaine has accepted my friend request. My mouth runs dry when I read his name. I had almost forgotten I had sent him one. Forgetting about the coffee, I sit down in my computer chair, ready to send him a message when I stop myself, fresh debate in my mind. Do I really want to talk with him again when I just saw him less than an hour ago?

You dragged that boy through Hell today. The least you can do is say hi, I tell myself.

I bring my hand to my mouth, gnawing lightly on the skin hanging off my thumb's cuticle in indecision. If I do message him, there's still a lot for us to discuss, like the stress website I had promised the link to, but I still can't remember the name of the website, even for all my trying. Never sending it to him would imply I don't care, wouldn't it? *Unless he's already forgotten all about it.* Either way, that's *not* the impression I want to give off. Sighing, I pull up my search history to scroll through my month's worth of websites and find the link and send it to him.

Done.

Blaine writes me back instantly.

Blaine: Hey ^.^

I stare at it, heart fluttering in my chest as I notice that in my message, I hadn't even bothered to add a greeting.

Erica: Hi
Blaine: What's up?

He's not asking about the link, I think and wonder again how to respond.

Erica: Not much.
I type it quickly and stare at it, hating how bland and simple it seems, how *lifeless.*
Erica: You?
Blaine: Same.
Erica: Did you click on the link I sent? It's for that website.
Blaine: No, I haven't. Hold on.

Five minutes later, I receive no response from him. *So much for that,* I think dejectedly.
A new message pops up then on my screen, causing my heart to lurch as badly as it had the first time Blaine messaged me.

Kara: Girl, what are you up to?

My heart crunches in disappointment as soon as I realize it isn't him. Then, I raise an eyebrow. Is this a white flag to our petty feud?

Erica: I talked to him.
Kara: Him who? Your hot little cashier boy?

I read the words but typed text is so cold, so flat, that I have no idea if she has an attitude or not.

Erica: Yes, we actually get along quite well.
Kara: So, how is he? ~wink~
Erica: Not *that* well!

Kara: Well, then it's clearly not well enough.

I laugh, positive that all our negative vibes are gone, and close the conversation, the petty little fight over as quickly as it had started without it ever even being acknowledged. There's an unread message in my thread with Blaine when I pull it back up.

Blaine: That's wonderful information. Thank you.

I bite my lip. Now *he's* giving off a professional vibe, and I'm not sure how to answer.

Erica: Anytime.

I stare at the message for a long time before hitting send. It seems like a way to end the conversation, but I don't want to push my luck and have him irritated with me by continuing a conversation he's lost interest in.

Nothing more pathetic than that.

Blaine: So, what are your plans for the rest of the day?

Now I'm clueless. That's not what I had expected, not at all.

Erica: Just hanging around the house.
Blaine: Good deal, me too.
Erica: And here I was thinking I'm a nerd.
Blaine: I can dig that. Nerds are cute.

My heart just about flatlines. Did he really just call me cute? *Play it off, play it down,* the voice in my head whispers. *Just say* something normal.

Erica: Oh, is that right? :D

I hate myself for it already. Why the emoticon? I'm not even sure. I clench my hands into fists so hard that the skin over my knuckles turns white as I wait for his response.

Blaine: Yep ;)

My heart is ready to explode in my chest. I had been so prepared for a negative response that the positive one sends me reeling. This relationship is really blossoming into something more than what coworkers share, and I'm on top of the world.

11.

THE NIGHT PASSES with me in a mood that's very *unlike* me, and as I pull into my usual parking spot at work the next day, the mood continues. Instead of anxiety, all I can think about is how seemingly perfect everything is. It's a strange contrast to the clouds inside of my mind the other day. *It'll be a good day,* I think, actually believing it, and wear a huge smile on my face that lasts all the way through the door.

When I get inside, however, it's a different story. Camilla is at the register and waves as I pass her to put my purse in my locker. I wave back, and when I return to the front, I reluctantly take my place at her side. It's Blaine's day off, but I'm actually relieved. I had barely been able to think up responses online and after support group, I had nearly choked on my own tongue. Now, with the new butterflies fluttering in my stomach, it would have been downright impossible to communicate coherently.

A blessing in disguise.

This is my first day manning my own register with Camilla here. I'm so used to being by her side that I have a tendency to look her way to see if she has something to tell me. I tell myself not to, but reflex reaction makes me distracted and it's not long before Camilla makes her way over to me.

She probably thinks I'm weird, I think, squeezing my eyes shut as I wait for her to speak.

"You're doing so well!" she gushes.

My eyes pop back open instantly—not what I had expected. but I'll take it anyway. Her finger points to the perfectly organized chips, and I feel my chest swell up with pride. Nothing like a mental defect to buy you compliments.

"Thanks," I say lamely, and before I have to worry about what to say other than that, she rushes off to compliment a customer on her outfit.

Maybe she just compliments everything, I resolve.

"Hey, girl!" Kara's voice calls to me.

I smile and turn to her. "What are you doing here?"

"Spying on you," she says. "After that juicy little nugget you gave me last night? I gotta have all the details! So. Where's your boy?"

"Shhh!!" I say, holding my hand up with a frantic glance to Camilla. "You can't just…*say* things like that. He's barely my friend, let alone anything else."

"Ah," she says, rolling her eyes. "Yet, he went with you to your group yesterday?"

I tense. "How did you know that?"

A wicked grin makes its way across her face. "I have my sources. But really, where is he?"

"He's off today." The words bring a new wave of depression as soon as they leave my mouth, and I wonder if he really had the day off or if he called out today *because* of yesterday.

"Too bad. I still expect a full report," she says, eyes furrowing.

I raise an eyebrow. "Of?"

Her mouth hangs open in exasperation. "Everything that's been going on. He added you on Facebook, right? Anything good on there?"

"How do you know things so *fast?*" I ask, setting my hands on the counter.

"If I'm not keeping up with your updates as they happen in real time, am I really even your best friend?"

I laugh and hold up my hands in defeat. "Okay, fair enough. Nothing…happened. I just talked to him a bit. Then we went home."

"That's definitely a start. Nerdy but respectable." Kara snaps on her gum again. "Anyway, before I hold you up much longer, I just wanted to see if you'd be up for getting drinks tonight. My treat."

I narrow my eyes. "Kara, nothing happened! Really!"

"We'll see if you stand by that after a couple of tequila shots," she says, tapping her hand on the shelf closest to her. "Come on! Please?"

I sigh, feeling myself lose every ounce of willpower I have

which, as it turns out, isn't much to begin with. "Fine, fine."

Kara squeals and claps her hands together, pulling Camilla's attention from the other register. "Fantastic!"

A half-smile makes its way to my face. "You got your way now, let me do my job before I get in trouble!"

She gives me her best fake menacing glare and takes a step away before sending me a fresh smile over her shoulder. "Deal. Now, don't stand me up!"

12.

AS DULL AS the day has been so far, at least I know I have art class to look forward to and then a night out with Kara. Who knows? She might actually be proud when she sees me this time.

As I organize the bags on my register, I hear someone set something down on the belt and turn to see Blaine. Instantly, my heart does its annoying thing and leaps up into the back of my throat. "Hi," I say, staring at him without even an attempt to reach for the bottle of water he had set down.

"Hey, so I have a question for you."

I raise an eyebrow. "What would that be?"

"How would you like me to bring you to your art class?" he asks.

I tilt my head to the side as I reach for his bottle and run it over the scanner. "How do you know it's today?"

"You can Google just about everything. I mean it *is* today, right?"

I nod uncertainly, and his smile returns.

"Then what do you say?"

TWENTY MINUTES LATER, I'm in Blaine's truck. He sits in the driver's seat, adjusting his mirror, and casts me a sideways smile as I look around the contents of his vehicle. It feels so intimate, being in such a small space, just him and me. He starts to drive, and I relax against the seat, though I continue to thread my fingers together nervously.

He asks me directions to my house, and when we pull up out front, I smile at him. "It'll be just a minute."

I rush inside, heart thrumming as I seek out my art tote and throw on another outfit—putting it on three times over, of course—before I rush back out to his truck. He glances at the bag on my lap as I pull the seatbelt into place.

"Do we have to bring our own supplies?" he asks.

I shake my head. "Viola provides them if we need them, but I like to carry my own."

He bobs his head. "Mind if I use yours too?"

"Not at all," I say, wondering if that's some type of compulsion of his or something else.

We flick the radio back and forth, looking for a good song to settle on as he pulls into the parking lot and stops the car.

"After you," he says, and I lead the way inside.

We're not the first ones, like I usually am, but Viola smiles at my appearance just the same. "Erica, dear! Good to see you again." Then she turns to Blaine. "And you are?"

"Blaine," he says, stretching out his hand for a handshake.

"Blaine, well, I'm Viola," she says, stretching her smile. "Go ahead and take a seat anywhere."

I obey, and Blaine takes the stool beside me. We take turns reaching into my art tote to pull out supplies that we spread across the table. When the classroom fills up, Viola gives a quick overview, and then we're left to begin our art. It's acrylic paints again that we're focusing on, and I already know the project I want to tackle—something bright and cheery. Not quite rainbows, since I had already pulled that off once, somehow, but something similar.

I start to paint, but Blaine sits rigidly beside me, watching me work. I've already got half of my canvas colored in some way when I glance at his blank one and stop.

"Are you okay?" I ask him.

"I'm not sure what to do," he admits.

I smile gently. "It's easy," I assure him. "Just paint what's in your head."

Blaine looks at my canvas again. "Your mind is cheerful then."

I wish. "Paint something."

"Okay," he says with a shrug and picks up a paintbrush, dabbing it with red paint that he flings at his canvas like a rock from a slingshot.

"That's a start," I say.

"Sure," he says with a laugh, and when he goes to pick up another blob, it falls off, landing on my shirt.

"Oh, my God! I'm sorry," he says, searching out a napkin but can't find anything even remotely similar nearby.

I stretch my hand out, not quite touching the stain, but fanning it slightly to urge it to dry as I say, "It's okay. It's just a casualty of art."

When he realizes I'm not angry, his panic relaxes, and he smiles at me, picking up his paintbrush once again.

13.

BLAINE PULLS UP outside of my house once again an hour later, and we sit in awkward silence for a few seconds that feel like forever.

"Today was fun," Blaine says at last, setting his brake to turn and look at me.

I smile and look down at the painting in my lap. It's Blaine's speckled canvas which I had agreed to hang onto, so it wouldn't be thrown around his backseat during the drive. Looking at it now, I find it hard to pry my fingers off of it.

"What's wrong?" he asks.

"I've grown attached to your painting," I admit with a small laugh.

He reaches out to lift up his work so that he can see my canvas underneath. "Yours is beautiful too, you know." He pauses. "How about we trade?"

I raise an eyebrow. "You want to keep my art?"

He shrugs. "Yeah, why not? It'll be nice to hang something up made by a real artist."

That causes me to blush. "I'm hardly—"

"Nonsense," he says before I can finish. "I just feel bad that you'll be stuck with my uh, *creation*."

I look at it again. "It's beautiful. Thank you."

"Anytime," he says.

I set my hand on the door, but I don't want to open it, don't want the moment to end.

Then he says, "Well, I guess I'll see you at work," and I know that's my cue to go.

"Bye," I reply and step out of the truck. I walk around it, inching up my foot trodden path in the snow as I hear him pull away. When I dash inside my house, my cheeks are burning though I can't tell if it's with hormones or cold. I turn the corner into my kitchen and gasp, catching sight of Kara sitting at my table. She looks up at me, eyes wide.

"There you are, girl! I thought you forgot," she says then looks at the canvas tucked under my arm. "Ooh, let Mama see!"

I hold out the canvas, wondering if she'll be able to tell it's not my work, and she studies the colors from one corner to the next. "This is beautiful."

"Thank you," I say in agreement and set it onto the table beside her as I study my walls for the perfect place to hang it.

She gathers the hammer and nails, frowning at the smudge of red paint on my shirt, and as soon as Blaine's painting is on the wall, she immediately drags me to my room to get a change of clothes. I owe Kara a thank you for her plan. Getting ready for the evening turns out to be a wonderful distraction from my obsessions—Blaine included. I pick out a red dress, take it off and put it back on three times over, and decide it's what I'm going to wear for the night. I barely even have time to blink before we're at the bar, drinks in front of us.

Kara's eyes are wide with excitement as she shoves the tiny cup full of tequila at me. "Cheers!" she says and downs hers.

A moment later, I do the same though a bit less eager. It burns the back of my throat and sits with a heavy feeling in the pit of my stomach, sending a spreading sensation of warmth across my chest. One drink leaves me faintly buzzed. Then, I realize my phone is buzzing too. I pull it out to see an IM from Blaine.

Blaine: I had a lot of fun hanging out with you today.
Erica: Me too.
Blaine: What do you have planned for the rest of the night?

My heart just about plummets to my stomach. Why does he want to know, and how do I answer without him getting the wrong impression of me?

Kara's impatient nails dig into my arm. "Earth to Erica! What've you got in your phone? Nudes?"

A blush lines my cheeks at the thought as I force my eyes away from the message. "No, I…" I trail off, still in shock that Blaine wants to talk to me *again* so soon after parting ways. I don't know why it comes as such a surprise. Maybe I've gotten too used to people running away at the first sign of my crazy that it's strange to see them come *back*.

Kara holds out her hand, palm up, and curls her fingers, looking at me through hooded eyes. "Let Mama see."

I pass it to her without question, though a voice in the back of my head wonders if that was really a good decision or not. A big grin crosses her face, and I know I've made a mistake. When she passes me back the phone, I read her response, cringing with every word.

"Erica:" Chillin' at home. Thinkin' about you, boo!

"He's gonna know this isn't me," I say, pointing to the phone in my hand.

Kara shrugs and puts away another shot. "Maybe. Maybe not. Let's see what happens," she says, pretending to eat an imaginary bucket of popcorn.

I frown. This is a game to her, purely entertainment, but to me it's important. Every second of this "game" makes me feel sick with uncertainty. I can't take my eyes off the phone as soon as the message says *read*. My heart feels ready to give out as I watch the dots dancing on the screen as Blaine types up his response. I wonder if the suspense from those dots has ever killed anyone.

Blaine: Haha! That right? Well, while we're being honest with one another, I've thought about you quite a bit too.

I blink and read the words three times over, but they don't seem real.

"Well, what'd he say?" Kara pouts, downing a third shot to accentuate her fake depression.

"He says he thinks about me too," I say, showing her the

message.

She reads it quickly, cat-like eyes darting back and forth before she looks over the phone at me and says, "Mazel tov! You might've hooked you a Ken doll."

I smirk as the phone buzzes again.

Blaine: This might seem out of the blue, and I understand if you say no, but would you maybe want to go see a movie or something?

That's the last thing I remember before looking into Kara's concerned face looming over me.

"Girl, you alright?" she asks, trying to peel back one of my eyelids to see if I'm conscious.

I groan in the back of my throat and my whole body alights with pain. "I…I'm…what happened?"

"You fainted. Fell right off the barstool."

"Well, that's embarrassing," I say, sitting up to survey the crowd that's gathered around me. It's an impressive number of people.

"Eh, you're fine," she says, checking the back of my head for lumps. "She's fine, everyone!" she repeats to the group who continue to watch on like vultures feeding on drama rather than death. They grumble to one another and eventually, begin to part. Kara turns back to me. "At the risk of fainting again, I went ahead and kept your boy busy." She passes me my phone.

My heart pounds at the memory of the last message I had read before my fainting spell mixed up my night, and I hold my breath, hoping to never do that again.

"Erica:" Of course! Anytime, anywhere.
Blaine: Cool. I've got some things in mind. Off tomorrow?
"Erica:" Yeah?
Blaine: I'll pick you up around 7.
"Erica:" That sounds wonderful.

"You got you a date, girly," Kara says, helping me back onto the barstool.

Another one, a voice in my head corrects. *One that has nothing to do with compulsions or obsessions. A normal date, the kind regular people go on.* My eyes are still on the phone as I murmur, "So it seems." I click it off but the message replays in my mind before a blush takes over my face.

14.

THE WORLD HAS a way of balancing—for every time something good happens, something bad has to happen and vice versa. With the thought of my date with Blaine, I mentally prepare myself for the blow of something bad that I'm sure is headed my way. I'm not prepared for how bad the actual outcome is and how quickly it comes to me. My phone buzzes, and I realize it's my *manager* calling.

My face deadpans and I'm glad that I've only had one shot. "Yes, sir?" I ask right as I answer the call.

"Erica, I'm afraid I have some bad news. Is there any way you can make a trip by the store? I'd rather talk about this in person."

I find it hard to swallow, and I wonder if it's actually physically possible to choke on your tongue. My mind races, trying to figure out what I've done wrong, but I can't pull up an answer. I haven't been late, I haven't missed a shift, and I've done my job exactly as Camilla had shown me to do.

"Y-yeah, sure," I say at last but in the back of my mind, I'm crying with panic. *I can't really be fired, can I?*

"Okay. I'll see you soon, Erica," he says, and the line goes dead as I listen to it.

Kara senses the change in my mood instantly. "What's wrong?"

My eyes well up with tears that make me feel truly pathetic as I reply, "My boss wants to talk to me."

"Uh-oh," Kara says.

The look on her face is too much to bear.

KARA IS FAR too drunk to drive. I do it even though I'm sure my nerves put us in just as much danger of an accident. We make it to the store with no incident, and I leave Kara in the car, cracking the window like she's a puppy. With my heart sending SOS signals all the way to my brain, I enter the store and hurry past the front, shielding my face with my hand. I don't even want Camilla to see me when I'm like this.

I rush to the back and breathe in deep, flashes of my last job in my mind, as I finally make it to the office and knock hesitantly on the door.

"Sir? You wanted to talk?" I ask, cracking the door just enough to pop my head inside.

Greg looks up from the papers on his desk and smiles grimly. Suddenly, I *miss* his shark-like grin more than anything. "Yes, Erica, please take a seat."

I obey and glance at the paper at the top of the pile—it's a chart of some kind.

"Before I begin, just know that this is a very difficult situation for me to approach," he says.

I nod as if I understand, even though I don't. My mind is still paralyzed with fear, waiting for him to drop his bad news on me, whatever it may be.

"You see, the store has been doing wonderfully since the holidays began, but after the recent few weeks, I see there's been a decline."

That sickening lump in my stomach feels stronger, like it's growing in size with each word he says. "So, how does that affect me?" I force myself to ask almost knowing the answer.

"Unfortunately, I'm not going to be able to provide you with the hours you need. I'll be able to spare maybe fifteen or twenty a week, but I can't offer full time, as I originally said I would. I am so sorry, Erica."

"That's…fine," I choke out feeling sick. Somehow, this is much worse than being fired. I can't pay my bills with such a low number of hours a week. I'll have to work two jobs…if I can even find another one willing to work with me for a schedule, that is.

"Are you okay?" he asks.

I don't answer. How can I when all the thoughts in my head are flying around at a ridiculously rapid pace? Instead, I give up trying and get up to walk away.

Kara is surprisingly sober by the time I get back to the car, and her eyes are wide with anticipation. "What happened?" she asks.

"Th-they're going to have to cut my hours. It's now going to be just a part-time position," I say, sticking the key in the ignition to avoid eye contact.

"They didn't fire you, though," she says as if I'm not already aware of that fact.

"No, but he might as well have. He said there was a decrease in profit, so he can't afford to have me."

"Oh, honey," Kara's face softens, and she sets a hand on my arm. "At least you still have something for now."

It occurs to me that she doesn't understand exactly *why* this is bad, and I don't have it in me to explain to her. "Yeah," I say, barely concealing my sigh.

OUTSIDE IN THE parking lot, I take my time plodding back to the car, letting the cold pierce through me just to try and regain myself. I look up, staring at the black sky, the only real evidence of night time. The lights from the city blur out the stars, but the ominous black of nothingness still looms overhead. Sometimes, I imagine it's what fills me up during my moments of self-hatred, that if maybe I could see the stars, then sometimes, the blackness wouldn't be so overwhelming, so all consuming.

But, we don't always get what we wish for. In fact, some never do.

I don't want to be around *anyone* right now, but I can't get rid of Kara to save my life. Even though she's quiet for the rest of the drive, she perks up once we get back to my house.

"I keep forgetting to tell you, but your lights are perfect," she says in way of compliment.

I can't smile, and I hide that fact from Kara by climbing out of the car. She is right behind me, frowning with her hand on my shoulder as we shuffle up the path to the house. Out of spite, I knock over the nearest light-up reindeer as we pass it.

"Hey, you've got your date tomorrow, still."

"Yeah," I say softly, eyes on the porch. It's a true statement, but I don't see it in the same light as I did an hour ago with tequila and happiness in my system.

Kara's frown twists back into a playful smile. "Do I need to give you the talk?"

I smile at her, but she can tell I don't mean it. So, she changes her approach.

"Hey," she says, wiping a strand of orange-red hair from my eyes. "Want to have a sleepover tonight? Like we did when we were kids?"

I don't know why she asked because she didn't mean it as a question. She's already decided. With an excited squeal, she goes to my bedroom and pulls out two pairs of pajamas—one for me and one for her. I gawk at the mess in the drawer, but Kara either doesn't notice or doesn't care because she pushes me to the bathroom to put on the clothes, and the next thing I know, we're sitting on the couch watching Snow White, Cinderella, and whatever other fairytales she can get her hands on.

Her presence helps, it does. It would almost be a good night.

Except, I can't stop thinking about my messed-up drawer.

15.

FOR THE REST of the night, every time my phone goes off, Kara insists on knowing who it is—she's practically glued to my hip for fear that I might get another phone call that will destroy this tiny cheer she's worked so hard to create in me. She's stubborn, and I love her for it.

The next morning comes before I can process it, and then it's time for my date. She dresses me—another thing I'm grateful for since it takes out another part of my usual routine. That is, until I get to the shoes. Kara hadn't planned that far ahead, surprisingly. When I manage to rummage through my choices, I feel sick. My mind is getting tied up at the thought. Every pair I have, I have to try on three times before tossing them aside. The longer I search, the worse I begin to feel.

It bothers me that I only put on my outfit once and even telling myself it's fine, that I'm okay, I can't shake the feeling away. Tears clot in the corners of my eyes, and I blink—three times, of course— to clear them. I pull off the dress and put it back on, but it doesn't feel right. I throw the nearest pair of shoes as the tears begin to flow down my face. Then I think of my mother and the way she used to console me even though I could see the disappointment in her eyes for the way I am.

I collapse onto my bed, burying my face in the covers.

The shoes are the straw that breaks the camel's back. As soon as they clatter to the floor, everything comes loose. I can't stop thinking of my compulsions telling me that I need to take the shoes off and put them back on two more times before I can be sure if they work or not. Unfortunately, my mind is very much like a chain, one thought looping to another until I'm back to hating myself for losing my original job when my life had been perfect.

I'm spiraling, so deep and so fast that I don't know how to get out. What's wrong with me that I can't even get ready for a *date*? This is new, and my body doesn't accept it. It isn't usual for me to get "stuck" in my rut but it happens occasionally, and I can't get out of it. Not on my own anyway.

Kara rushes to my side, murmuring sympathetic words in my ear as her hand presses to my back, but I hardly notice. All I can think is that I'm a blubbering mess, and I'll have to cancel the date—*why would Blaine even want to date me to begin with*—and when he finds out the reason, *if* he does, he might never talk to me again. He had seemed disgusted enough with his own obsessive tendencies that I doubt he'll have the patience to deal with mine.

Sniffling, I lift my hand to wipe away the layer of tears and snot on my face before reaching pathetically for my phone.

Kara's eyes grow wide. "Girl, don't do it. Just take a breath and cool off, and we'll try something else, okay?"

I don't acknowledge her as I pull up the conversation with Blaine, sniffling again when I quickly skim over our last few messages before sending him a brand new one.

Erica: I can't make our date.

I turn off the phone as soon as it sends. I don't want to read his response.

16.

I CRY MYSELF to sleep, so wrapped up in self-hatred that I can't even show my face to the light of my bedroom. When I wake up, I realize Kara is curled next to me, dead asleep. She didn't move an inch all night. I smile at the top of her blonde head as I stand up, wiping at my puffy, swollen face. For all her craziness, she can be sweet sometimes. Remembering my predicament makes the happiness short-lived. On shaky legs, I approach the pile of shoes and clothes, going through the same wave of despair that I had the previous night, though with less intensity.

I strip off my clothes again and look for pajamas to pull on, but everything is everywhere, and my despair is overwhelming once more. I drop to my knees, digging through the few outfits left in my drawer before I find my pajamas. I wipe my eyes with the back of my hand and breathe a sigh of relief as I slip them on, feeling the hold of my compulsion clear away.

I glance at Kara on the bed, but she's still sound asleep. Then, I catch sight of my cellphone in the bed beside her and remember—Blaine and the canceled date. The thought comes to me like a punch to the stomach. Winded, I rush to scoop up the damn device and turn it on, watching the screen come to life. As the home screen loads, I find myself holding my breath. A moment later, a notification pings in my phone and I don't have to look to know what it is—Blaine's response. Through narrowed eyes, I swipe open the phone and read it.

Blaine: Why're you standing me up?

My throat tightens and suddenly it doesn't matter how much better I felt a moment ago, I'm back at the bottom of the pit now, beneath the dirt and stones, just as low as I can possibly go, and I have that urge to start crying all over again. I stare at the message, pondering what to do. I can't ignore the situation I've created. Better to get it over with quickly, like tearing off a band-aid.

Erica: Want the truth?
Blaine: Yes.

I blink and stare at the single word. So cold, so precise…so impossible to guess what he's thinking.

Erica: When I was getting ready for our date, everything I've been dealing with hit me and I-I got stuck and couldn't pull myself out of it. I tried for hours but…nothing worked. I'm so sorry.

That punch to my stomach is back again as I hit send. I barely let myself think of what I've just written—it's a risky text if I've ever sent one before. A long minute passes and another. Suddenly, my grief and uncertainty hardens to anger. How dare he? Who is *he* to judge me in my moment of despair? I had opened up to him, showed him a side of myself that makes me feel insignificant, and he takes it as a sign of weakness? I feel so used that I'm ready to throw my phone against the wall when I realize it's buzzing with his response.

Blaine: Really, sweetheart? I owe you an apology.

My heart. It catches in my throat, and I feel guilty for the anger, for how quick I was to assume that he was a bad guy, impossible of understanding.

Blaine: When you wrote me that message last night, I was so mad at you. I thought you changed your mind…because of everything you know about me, and I wanted to hate you for getting my hopes up. You should've just told me the truth, what was really going on. Like you told me, our compulsions are nothing to be ashamed of. I would've come over in a heartbeat to help. And if our date is what caused it, I would've said we could hang at your place if you wanted! No problem.

Stunned, I collapse onto the bed next to Kara's *still* sleeping form, heart full of more emotion than I'm comfortable with. This boy, this person who only a week ago had been a stranger to me, could very well be my other half, building me up in the places I'm determined to tear down.

I can't contain my surprise and get up again, walking into the bathroom.

Erica: Really?
Blaine: Yes. I'm gonna be brutally honest with you. I like you. I wouldn't have told you the truth about me if I didn't.

I think of Camilla on my first day, talking of Blaine's "mysteriousness" and I know he's telling the truth. That brings a smile back to my face. My fingers clench onto the sink, and I find myself grinning stupidly at my reflection, the bad vibes from the incident already long forgotten.

Blaine: Let's go get some coffee, my treat.
Erica: Sure thing.

I set my phone down to splash water on my face and hear it rumble with his response.

Blaine: <3

In the back of my mind, I can hear Blaine's voice. *It's like the OCD games or something,* he had said. In a way, he's right. For once, I'm not frustrated as I go to wash my face for the third time that minute. For better or for worse, I am who I am. Every time I get to a point where I don't think people can surprise me anymore, they do. They always do. As I stand, grinning stupidly at my reflection and wiping bitter tears off my face, I don't expect to hear a knock.

At first, I assume it's Kara getting up, searching for me, but when I go back to my room, I confirm that she's still lying there, curled on the bed. Instantly, my face crunches in confusion as soon as the sound rings out again. Then I realize it's coming from the *door.* I wipe at my puffy, swollen eyes with the back of my hand and see the smudges of mascara on my skin.

I barely pay attention to it as I approach my front door. The knocking sounds again, more confident than before and I throw the door open, fully ready for whatever kind of confrontation waits on the other side.

Then I freeze as I realize it's *Blaine.*

His hair is tucked under a red beanie which leaves his eyes to appear enormous in the low light. He smiles at me sheepishly, holding up a small sprig of mistletoe high up in the air. A few snowflakes cling to the crisp green thing, making it look like a plastic decoration because beauty like that is hard to maintain for real.

My eyes travel from the mistletoe to Blaine's face.

He doesn't speak, just gives me time to observe the scene. "You know what they say about mistletoe," he says so softly that I almost don't hear him say it.

I laugh, and tiny twin tears fall from the opposite corners of my eyes. I don't give him a chance to say anything else before I throw my arms around his shoulders and press my lips to his. I hear the soft thump as the mistletoe meets the snow, and he pulls me tighter into his embrace.

In that moment, I feel whole. It's as if the parts of who we are, the pieces that aren't affected by our compulsions are singing, happy to have found one another. When we break apart, we're both smiling with the warmth of new affection flushing our faces.

As I stand here, staring into Blaine's face, I know one thing is for sure: I'm going to be just fine.

About the Author

Kayla Krantz is fascinated by the dark and macabre. Stephen King is her all-time inspiration mixed in with a little bit of Eminem and some faint remnants of the works of Edgar Allen Poe. When she began writing, she started in horror but somehow drifted into thriller. She loves the 1988 movie Heathers. Kayla was born and raised in Michigan but traveled across the country to where she currently resides in Texas.

She has ideas for books in many genres which she hopes to write and publish in the future.

http://www.facebook.com/kaylakrantzwriter/
https://twitter.com/kaylathewriter9
https://authorkaylakrantz.com/